"But why—but why should any wish to kill me?" said Mowgli.

"Look at me," said Bagheera. And Mowgli looked at him steadily between the eyes. The big panther turned his head away in half a minute.

"That is why," he said, shifting his paw on the leaves. "Not even I can look thee between the eyes, and I was born among men, and I love thee, Little Brother. The others they hate thee because their eyes cannot meet thine; because thou art wise; because thou hast pulled out thorns from their feet—because thou art a man."

THE JUNGLE BOOK

RUDYARD KIPLING

Edited by Barbara Solot

Afterword by Beth Johnson

 THE TOWNSEND LIBRARY

THE JUNGLE BOOK

TP THE TOWNSEND LIBRARY

For more titles in the Townsend Library,
visit our website: **www.townsendpress.com**

All new material in this edition is
copyright © 2003 by Townsend Press.
Printed in the United States of America

0 9 8 7 6 5 4 3

Townsend Press, Inc.
1038 Industrial Drive
West Berlin, New Jersey 08091

ISBN 1-59194-008-7

Library of Congress Control Number:
2003100036

TABLE OF CONTENTS

CHAPTER 1

It was seven o'clock on a very warm evening in the Seeonee hills when Father Wolf woke up from his day's rest, scratched himself, yawned, and spread out his paws one after the other to get rid of the sleepy feeling in their tips. Mother Wolf lay with her big gray nose dropped across her four tumbling, squealing cubs, and the moon shone into the mouth of the cave where they all lived. *"Augrh!"* said Father Wolf. "It is time to hunt again." He was going to spring down hill when a little shadow with a bushy tail crossed the threshold and whined: "Good luck go with you,

O Chief of the Wolves. And good luck and strong white teeth go with your noble children that they may never forget the hungry in this world."

It was the jackal—Tabaqui. The wolves of India despise Tabaqui because he runs about making mischief, and telling tales, and eating rags and pieces of leather from the village rubbish-heaps. But they are afraid of him too, because Tabaqui, more than anyone else in the jungle, is apt to go mad, and then he forgets that he was ever afraid of anyone. He runs through the forest biting everything in his way. Even the tiger runs and hides when little Tabaqui goes mad, for madness is the most disgraceful thing that can overtake a wild creature. We call it hydrophobia—or rabies—but they call it *dewanee*—the madness—and they run.

"Enter, then, and look," said Father Wolf stiffly, "but there is no food here."

"For a wolf, no," said Tabaqui, "but for so mean a person as myself a dry bone is a good feast. Who are we, the Gidur-log [the jackal people], to pick and choose?" He scuttled to the back of the cave, where he found the bone of a buck with some meat on it, and sat cracking the end merrily.

"All thanks for this good meal," he said, licking his lips. "How beautiful are your noble children! How large are their eyes! And so young too! Indeed, indeed, I might have remembered that the children of kings are men from the beginning."

Now, Tabaqui knew as well as anyone else that there is nothing so unlucky as to compliment children to their faces. It pleased him to see Mother and Father Wolf look uncomfortable.

Tabaqui sat still, rejoicing in the mischief that he had made, and then he said spitefully: "Shere Khan, the Big One, has shifted his hunting grounds. He will hunt among these hills for the next moon, so he has told me."

Shere Khan was the tiger who lived near the Waingunga River, twenty miles away.

"He has no right!" Father Wolf began angrily. "By the Law of the Jungle he has no right to change his quarters without due warning. He will frighten every head of game within ten miles, and I—I have to kill for two, these days."

"His mother did not call him Lungri [the Lame One] for nothing," said Mother Wolf quietly. "He has been lame in one foot from his birth. That is why he has only killed cattle.

Now the villagers of the Waingunga are angry with him, and he has come here to make our villagers angry. They will scour the jungle for him when he is far away, and we and our children must run when the grass is set on fire. Indeed, we are very grateful to Shere Khan!"

"Shall I tell him of your gratitude?" said Tabaqui.

"Out!" snapped Father Wolf. "Out and hunt with thy master. Thou hast done harm enough for one night."

"I'll go," said Tabaqui quietly. "Ye can hear Shere Khan below in the thickets. I might have saved myself the message."

Father Wolf listened, and below in the valley that ran down to a little river he heard the dry, angry, snarling, singsong whine of a tiger who has caught nothing and does not care if all the jungle knows it.

"The fool!" said Father Wolf. "To begin a night's work of hunting with that noise! Does he think that our buck are foolish?"

"H'sh. It is neither bullock nor buck he hunts tonight," said Mother Wolf. "It is Man."

The whine had changed to a sort of humming purr that seemed to come from every direction. It is a noise that bewilders woodcutters and gypsies sleeping in the open, and makes them run, sometimes right into the very mouth of the tiger.

"Man!" said Father Wolf, showing all his white teeth. "*Faugh!* Are there not enough beetles and frogs in the forest that he must eat Man, and on our ground too!"

The Law of the Jungle, which never orders anything without a reason, forbids every beast to eat Man except when he is killing to show his children how to kill, and then he must hunt outside the hunting grounds of his pack or tribe. The real reason for this is that man-killing means, sooner or later, the arrival of white men on elephants, with guns, and hundreds of brown men with gongs and rockets and torches. Then everybody in the jungle suffers. The reason the beasts give among themselves is that Man is the weakest and most defenseless of all living things, and it is unsportsmanlike to touch him. They say too—and it is true —that man-eaters become mangy and lose their teeth.

The purr grew louder, and ended in the full-throated *"Aaarh!"* of the tiger's charge.

Then there was a howl—an untigerish howl—from Shere Khan. "He has missed," said Mother Wolf. "What is it?"

Father Wolf ran out a few paces and heard

Shere Khan muttering and mumbling savage-
ly as he tumbled about in the scrub.

"The fool has had no more sense than to
jump at a woodcutter's campfire. He has
burned his feet," said Father Wolf with a
grunt. "Tabaqui is with him."

"Something is coming uphill," said
Mother Wolf, twitching one ear. "Get ready."

The bushes rustled a little in the thicket,
and Father Wolf dropped with his haunches
under him, ready for his leap. Then, if you
had been watching, you would have seen the
most wonderful thing in the world—the wolf
checked in mid-spring. He made his bound
before he saw what it was he was jumping at,
and then he tried to stop himself. The result
was that he shot up straight into the air for
four or five feet, landing almost where he left
ground.

"Man!" he snapped. "A man's cub.
Look!"

Directly in front of him, holding on by a
low branch, stood a naked brown baby who
could just walk—as soft and as dimpled a little being as ever came to a wolf's cave at
night. He looked up into Father Wolf's face
and laughed.

"Is that a man's cub?" said Mother Wolf.

"I have never seen one. Bring it here."

A Wolf accustomed to moving his own cubs can, if necessary, carry an egg in his mouth without breaking it, and though Father Wolf's jaws closed right on the child's back, not a tooth even scratched the skin as he laid it down among the cubs.

"How little! How naked, and—how bold!" said Mother Wolf softly. The baby was pushing his way between the cubs to get close to the warm hide. "*Ahai!* He is taking his meal with the others. So this is a man's cub. Now, was there ever a wolf that could boast of a man's cub among her children?"

"I have heard now and again of such a

thing, but never in our Pack or in my time," said Father Wolf. "He is altogether without hair, and I could kill him with a touch of my foot. But see, he looks up and is not afraid."

The moonlight was blocked out of the mouth of the cave, for Shere Khan's great square head and shoulders were thrust into the entrance. Tabaqui, behind him, was squeaking: "My lord, my lord, it went in here!"

"Shere Khan does us great honor," said Father Wolf, but his eyes were very angry. "What does Shere Khan need?"

"My prey. A man's cub went this way," said Shere Khan. "Its parents have run off. Give it to me."

Shere Khan had jumped at a woodcutter's campfire, as Father Wolf had said, and was furious from the pain of his burned feet. But Father Wolf knew that the mouth of the cave was too narrow for a tiger to come in by. Even where he was, Shere Khan's shoulders and forepaws were cramped for want of room, as a man's would be if he tried to fight in a barrel.

"The Wolves are a free people," said Father Wolf. "They take orders from the Head of the Pack, and not from any striped cattle-killer. The man's cub is ours—to kill if we choose."

"Ye choose and ye do not choose! How dare you talk of choosing? By the bull that I killed, I stand nosing into your den to get what's due to me? It is I, Shere Khan, who speak!"

The tiger's roar filled the cave with thunder. Mother Wolf shook herself clear of the cubs and sprang forward, her eyes, like two green moons in the darkness, facing the blazing eyes of Shere Khan.

"And it is I, Raksha [The Demon], who answers. The man's cub is mine! He shall not be killed. He shall live to run with the Pack and to hunt with the Pack; and in the end, O hunter of little naked cubs—frog-eater— fish-killer—he shall hunt thee! Now go—go back to thy mother, burned beast of the jungle, lamer than thou came into the world! Go!"

Father Wolf looked on amazed. He had almost forgotten the days when he won Mother Wolf in a fair fight from five other wolves, when she ran in the Pack and was called The Demon for good reason. Shere Khan might have faced Father Wolf, but he could not stand up against Mother Wolf, for he knew that where he was she had all the advantage of being on her home ground, and would fight to the death. So he backed out of the cave mouth growling, and when he was clear, he shouted:

"We will see what the Pack will say to this fostering of man-cubs. The cub is mine, and to my teeth he will come in the end, O bush-tailed thieves!"

Mother Wolf threw herself down panting among the cubs, and Father Wolf said to her gravely:

"Shere Khan speaks the truth. The cub must be shown to the Pack. Will thou still keep him, Mother?"

"Keep him!" she gasped. "He came naked, by night, alone and very hungry; yet he was not afraid! Look, he has pushed one of my babes to one side already. And that lame butcher would have killed him and then run off to the Waingunga while the villagers here hunted through all our lairs in revenge! Keep him? Assuredly I will keep him. Lie still, little frog. O thou Mowgli —for Mowgli the Frog I will call thee—the time will come when thou will hunt Shere Khan as he has hunted thee."

"But what will our Pack say?" said Father Wolf.

The Law of the Jungle lays down very clearly that any wolf may, when he marries, withdraw from the Pack he belongs to. But as soon as his cubs are old enough to stand on their feet, he must bring them to the Pack Council, which is generally held once a month at full moon, in order that the other wolves may identify them. After that inspection the cubs are free to run where they please, and until they have killed their first buck, no excuse is accepted if a grown wolf of the Pack kills one of them. The punishment is death if the murderer can be found; and if you think about this for a minute, you will see that this must be so.

Father Wolf waited till his cubs could run a little, and then on the night of the Pack Meeting took them and Mowgli and Mother Wolf to the Council Rock—a hilltop covered with stones and boulders where a hundred wolves could hide. Akela, the great gray Lone Wolf, who led all the Pack by strength and cunning, lay out at full length on his rock. Below him sat forty or more wolves of every size and color, from older badger-colored veterans who could handle a buck alone to young black three-year-olds who thought they could. The Lone Wolf had led them for a year now. He had fallen into a wolf trap twice in his youth, and once he had been beaten and left for dead; so he knew the manners and customs of men. There was very little talking at the Rock. The cubs tumbled over each other in the center of the circle where their mothers and fathers sat, and now and again a senior wolf would go quietly up to a cub, look at him carefully, and return to his place on noiseless feet. Sometimes a mother would push her cub far out into the moonlight to be sure that he had not been overlooked. Akela from his rock would cry: "Ye know the Law—ye know the Law. Look well, O Wolves!" And the anxious mothers would take up the call: "Look—look well, O Wolves!"

At last—and Mother Wolf's neck bristles lifted as the time came—Father Wolf pushed "Mowgli the Frog," as they called him, into the center, where he sat laughing and playing with some pebbles that glistened in the moonlight.

Akela never raised his head from his paws, but went on with the monotonous cry: "Look well!" A muffled roar came up from behind the rocks—the voice of Shere Khan crying: "The cub is mine. Give him to me. What have the Free People to do with a man's cub?" Akela never even twitched his ears. All he said was: "Look well, O Wolves! What have we, the Free People, to do with the orders of any except the Free People? Look well!"

There was a chorus of deep growls, and a young wolf in his fourth year flung back Shere Khan's question to Akela: "What have the Free People to do with a man's cub?" Now, the Law of the Jungle lays down that if there is any dispute as to the right of a cub to be accepted by the Pack, he must be spoken for by at least two members of the Pack who are not his father and mother.

"Who speaks for this cub?" said Akela. "Among the Free People, who speaks?" There was no answer, and Mother Wolf got ready for what she knew would be her last fight, if things came to fighting.

Then, Baloo, the only other creature who is allowed at the Pack Council, rose up on his hind quarters and grunted. Baloo is the sleepy brown bear who teaches the wolf cubs the Law of the Jungle—old Baloo, who can come and go where he pleases because he eats only nuts and roots and honey.

"The man's cub—the man's cub?" he said. "I speak for the man's cub. There is no harm in a man's cub. I am not good with words, but I speak the truth. Let him run with the Pack and be entered with the others. I myself will teach him."

"We need yet another," said Akela. "Baloo has spoken, and he is our teacher for the young cubs. Who speaks besides Baloo?"

A black shadow dropped down into the circle. It was Bagheera the Black Panther, inky black all over, but with the panther markings showing up in certain lights like the pattern of watered silk. Everybody knew Bagheera, and nobody cared to cross his path, for he was as cunning as Tabaqui, as bold as the wild buffalo, and as reckless as the wounded elephant. But he had a voice as soft as wild honey dripping from a tree, and a skin softer than down.

"O Akela, and ye the Free People," he purred, "I have no right in your assembly, but the Law of the Jungle says that if there is a doubt which is not a matter of killing in regard to a new cub, the life of that cub may be bought at a price. And the Law does not say who may or may not pay that price. Am I right?"

"Good! Good!" said the young wolves, who are always hungry. "Listen to Bagheera. The cub can be bought for a price. It is the Law."

"Knowing that I have no right to speak here, I ask your permission."

"Speak then," cried twenty voices.

"To kill a naked cub is a shame. Besides, he may make better sport for you when he is grown. Baloo has spoken in his behalf. Now to Baloo's word I will add one bull, and a fat one, newly killed, not half a mile from here, if ye will accept the man's cub according to the Law. Do you accept this?"

There was a clamor of scores of voices, saying: "Why not? He will die in the winter rains. He will scorch in the sun. What harm can a naked frog do us? Let him run with the Pack. Where is the bull, Bagheera? Let him be accepted." And then came Akela's deep bay, crying: "Look well—look well, O Wolves!"

Mowgli was still deeply interested in the pebbles, and he did not notice when the wolves came and looked at him one by one. At last they all went down the hill for the dead bull, and only Akela, Bagheera, Baloo, and Mowgli's own wolves were left. Shere Khan roared in the still night, for he was very angry that Mowgli had not been handed over to him.

"Ay, roar well," said Bagheera, under his whiskers, "for the time will come when this naked thing will make thee roar to another tune, or I know nothing of Man."

"This was done well," said Akela. "Men and their cubs are very wise. He may be a help in time."

"Truly, a help in time of need, for none can hope to lead the Pack forever," said Bagheera.

Akela said nothing. He was thinking of the time that comes to every leader of every pack when his strength goes from him and he gets feebler and feebler, till at last he is killed by the wolves and a new leader comes up—to be killed in his turn.

"Take him away," he said to Father Wolf,

"and train him as befits one of the Free People."

And that is how Mowgli was entered into the Seeonee Wolf Pack for the price of a bull and on Baloo's good word.

Now you must be content to skip ten or eleven whole years, and only guess at the wonderful life that Mowgli led among the wolves, because if it were written out it would fill ever so many books. He grew up with the cubs, though they, of course, were grown wolves almost before he was a child. And Father Wolf taught him his business, and the meaning of things in the jungle, till every rustle in the grass, every breath of the warm night air, every note of the owls above his head, every scratch of a bat's claws as it roosted for a while in a tree, and every splash of every little fish jumping in a pool meant just as much to him as the work of his office means to a businessman.

When he was not learning, he sat out in the sun and slept and ate and went to sleep again. When he felt dirty or hot, he swam in the forest pools; and when he wanted honey (Baloo told him that honey and nuts were just as pleasant to eat as raw meat), he climbed up for it as Bagheera showed him how to do. Bagheera would lie out on a branch and call, "Come along, Little Brother." At first Mowgli would cling like the sloth, but afterward he would fling himself through the branches almost as boldly as the gray ape. He took his place at the Council Rock, too, when the Pack met, and there he discovered that if he stared hard at any wolf, the wolf would be forced to drop his eyes, and so he used to stare for fun.

At other times he would pick the long thorns out of the pads of his friends, for wolves suffer terribly from thorns and burs in their coats. He would go down the hillside into the cultivated lands at night, and look very curiously at the villagers in their huts, but he had a mistrust of men because Bagheera showed him a square box with a drop gate so cunningly hidden in the jungle that he nearly walked into it, and told him that it was a trap. Better than anything else, he loved to go with Bagheera into the dark warm heart of the forest, to sleep all through the drowsy day, and at night see how Bagheera did his killing. Bagheera killed right and left as he felt hungry, and so did Mowgli—with one exception.

As soon as he was old enough to understand, Bagheera told him that he must never touch cattle because he had been bought into the Pack at the price of a bull's life. "All the jungle is thine," said Bagheera, "and thou can kill everything that thou art strong enough to kill; but in honor of the bull that bought thee, thou must never kill or eat any cattle young or old. That is the Law of the Jungle." Mowgli obeyed faithfully.

And he grew and grew strong as a boy must grow who has nothing in the world to think about except what to eat. All the while, he learned many lessons without knowing he was learning.

Mother Wolf told him once or twice that Shere Khan was not a creature to be trusted, and that some day he must kill Shere Khan. But though a young wolf would have remembered that advice every hour, Mowgli forgot it because he was only a boy—though he would have called himself a wolf if he had been able to speak in any human tongue.

Shere Khan was always crossing his path in the jungle, for as Akela grew older and feebler, the lame tiger had come to be great friends with the younger wolves of the Pack, who followed him to pick up scraps of food. Akela would never have allowed this friendship if he had dared to exercise his authority to the proper bounds. Then Shere Khan would flatter the wolves and wonder that such fine young hunters were content to be led by a dying wolf and a man's cub. "They tell me," Shere Khan would say, "that at Council ye dare not look him between the eyes." And the young wolves would growl and bristle.

Bagheera, who had eyes and ears everywhere, heard about this, and once or twice he told Mowgli in so many words that Shere Khan would kill him some day. Mowgli would laugh and answer: "I have the Pack and I have thee; and Baloo, though he is so lazy, might strike a blow or two for my sake. Why should I be afraid?"

It was one very warm day that a new notion came to Bagheera— born of something that he had heard. Perhaps Sahi the Porcupine had told him; but when they were deep in the jungle, he said to Mowgli as the boy lay with his head on Bagheera's beautiful black skin, "Little Brother, how often have I told thee that Shere Khan is thy enemy?"

"As many times as there are nuts on that palm," said Mowgli, who, naturally, could not count. "What of it? I am sleepy, Bagheera, and

Shere Khan is all long tail and loud talk—like Mao, the Peacock."

"But this is no time for sleeping. Baloo knows it; I know it; the Pack know it; and even the foolish, foolish deer know. Tabaqui has told thee, too."

"Ho! ho!" said Mowgli. "Tabaqui came to me not long ago with some rude talk, saying that I was a naked man's cub and not fit to dig pig-nuts. But I caught Tabaqui by the tail and swung him twice against a palm tree to teach him better manners."

"That was foolishness, for though Tabaqui is a mischief-maker, he told thee of something that is a serious concern. Open those eyes, Little Brother. Shere Khan dare not kill thee in the jungle. But remember, Akela is very old, and soon the day will come when he cannot kill his buck, and then he will be leader no more. Many of the wolves that looked thee over when thou was first brought to the Council are old too, and the young wolves believe, as Shere Khan has taught them, that a man-cub has no place with the Pack. In a little time thou will be a man."

"And what is a man that he should not run with his brothers?" said Mowgli. "I was born in the jungle. I have obeyed the Law of the Jungle, and there is no wolf of ours from whose paws I have not pulled a thorn. Surely they are my brothers!"

Bagheera stretched himself at full length and half shut his eyes. "Little Brother," he said, "feel under my jaw."

Mowgli put up his strong brown hand, and just under Bagheera's silky chin, where the giant rolling muscles were all hid by the glossy hair, he came upon a little bald spot.

"There is no one in the jungle that knows that I, Bagheera, carry that mark—the mark of the collar. And yet, Little Brother, I was born among men, and it was among men that my mother died—in the cages of the king's palace at Oodeypore. It was because of this that I paid the price for thee at the Council when thou was a little naked cub. Yes, I too was born among men. I had never seen the jungle. They fed me behind bars from an iron pan till one night I felt that I was Bagheera—the Panther—and no man's plaything, and I broke the silly lock with one blow of my paw and ran away. And because I had learned the ways of men, I became more terrible in the jungle than Shere Khan. Is it not so?"

"Yes," said Mowgli, "all in the jungle fear Bagheera—all except Mowgli."

"Oh, thou art a man's cub," said the Black Panther very tenderly. "And as I returned to my jungle, so thou must go back to men at last—to the men who are thy brothers—if thou art not killed in the Council."

"But why—but why should any wish to kill me?" said Mowgli.

"Look at me," said Bagheera. And Mowgli looked at him steadily between the eyes. The big panther turned his head away in half a minute.

"That is why," he said, shifting his paw on the leaves. "Not even I can look thee between the eyes, and I was born among men, and I love thee, Little Brother. The others they hate thee because their eyes cannot meet thine; because thou art wise; because thou hast pulled out thorns from their feet—because thou art a man."

"I did not know these things," said Mowgli sullenly, frowning under his heavy black eyebrows.

"What is the Law of the Jungle? Strike first and then speak. By thy very carelessness they know that thou art a man. But be wise. It is in my heart that when Akela misses his next kill—and at each hunt it becomes harder for him to pin the buck—the Pack will turn against him and against thee. They will hold a jungle Council at the Rock, and then—and then . . . I have it!" said Bagheera, leaping up. "Go down quickly to the men's huts in the valley, and take some of the Red Flower which they grow there, so that when the time comes thou may have even a stronger friend than I or Baloo or those of the Pack that love thee. Get the Red Flower."

By Red Flower Bagheera meant fire, for no creature in the jungle will call fire by its proper name. Every beast lives in deadly fear of it, and invents a hundred ways of describing it.

"The Red Flower?" said Mowgli. "That grows outside their huts in the twilight. I will get some."

"Spoken like a man's cub," said Bagheera proudly. "Remember that it grows in little pots. Get one swiftly, and keep it by thee for time of need."

"Good!" said Mowgli. "I go. But art thou sure, O my Bagheera"—he slipped his arm around the splendid neck and looked deep into the big eyes—"art thou sure that all this is Shere Khan's doing?"

"By the Broken Lock that freed me, I am sure, Little Brother."

"Then, by the Bull that bought me, I will pay back Shere Khan in full for this, and maybe a little over," said Mowgli, and he bounded away.

"That is a man. That is all a man," said Bagheera to himself, lying down again. "Oh, Shere Khan, never have you made a bigger mistake than hunting the man-cub ten years ago!"

Mowgli ran far through the forest, running hard, his heart pounding inside him. He came to the cave as the evening mist rose, took a breath, and looked down the valley. The cubs were out, but Mother Wolf, at the back of the cave, knew by his breathing that something was troubling her frog.

"What is it, Son?" she said.

"Some bat's chatter about Shere Khan," he called back. "I hunt among the plowed fields tonight," and he plunged downward through the bushes, to the stream at the bottom of the valley. There he stopped, for he heard the yell of the Pack hunting, and he heard the bellow of a hunted buck, and the snort as the buck turned at bay. Then there were wicked, bitter howls from the young wolves: "Akela! Akela! Let the Lone Wolf show his strength. Room for the leader of the

Pack! Spring, Akela!"

The Lone Wolf must have sprung and missed his hold, for Mowgli heard the snap of his teeth and then a yelp as the buck knocked him over with his forefoot.

He did not wait for anything more, but dashed on; and the yells grew fainter behind him as he ran into the croplands where the villagers lived.

"Bagheera spoke the truth," he panted, as he nestled down in some straw by the window of a hut. "Tomorrow is a big day both for Akela and for me."

Then he pressed his face close to the window and watched the fire on the hearth. He saw the man's wife get up and feed it in the night with black lumps. And when the morning came and the mists were all white and cold, he saw the man's child pick up a wicker pot plastered inside with earth, fill it with lumps of red-hot charcoal, put it under his blanket, and go out to tend the cows in the barn.

"Is that all?" said Mowgli. "If a cub can do it, there is nothing to fear." So he strode round the corner and met the boy, took the pot from his hand, and disappeared into the mist while the boy howled with fear.

"They are very like me," said Mowgli,

blowing into the pot as he had seen the woman do. "This thing will die if I do not give it things to eat"; and he dropped twigs and dried bark on the red stuff. Halfway up the hill he met Bagheera with the morning dew shining like moonstones on his coat.

"Akela has missed," said the Panther. "They would have killed him last night, but they needed thee also. They were looking for thee on the hill."

"I was among the plowed lands. I am ready. See!" Mowgli held up the fire pot.

"Good! Now, I have seen men thrust a dry branch into that stuff, and presently the Red Flower blossomed at the end of it. Art thou not afraid?"

"No. Why should I fear? I remember now—if it is not a dream—how, before I was a Wolf, I lay beside the Red Flower, and it was warm and pleasant."

All that day Mowgli sat in the cave tending his fire pot and dipping dry branches into it to see how they looked. He found a branch that satisfied him, and in the evening when Tabaqui came to the cave and rudely told him that he was wanted at the Council Rock, he laughed 'til Tabaqui ran away. Then Mowgli went to the Council, still laughing.

Akela the Lone Wolf lay by the side of his rock as a sign that the leadership of the Pack was open, and Shere Khan with his following of scrap-fed wolves walked to and fro. Bagheera lay close to Mowgli, and the fire-pot was between Mowgli's knees. When they were all gathered together, Shere Khan began to speak—a thing he would never have dared to do when Akela was in his prime.

"He has no right to speak," whispered Bagheera. "Say so and he will be frightened."

Mowgli sprang to his feet. "Free People," he cried, "does Shere Khan lead the Pack? What has a tiger to do with our leadership?"

"Seeing that the leadership is yet open, and being asked to speak—" Shere Khan began.

"Who asks you to speak?" said Mowgli. "Are we all jackals, to fawn on this cattle butcher? The leadership of the Pack is with the Pack alone."

There were yells of "Silence, thou man's cub!" "Let him speak. He has kept our Law"; and at last the seniors of the Pack thundered: "Let the Dead Wolf speak." When a leader of the Pack has missed his kill, he is called the Dead Wolf as long as he lives, which is not long.

Akela raised his old head wearily:

"Free People, and ye too, jackals of Shere Khan, for twelve seasons I have led ye to and from the kill, and in all that time not one has been trapped or maimed. Now I have missed my kill. Ye know how that happened. Ye know how ye brought me up to an untried buck to make my weakness known. It was cleverly done. Your right is to kill me here on the Council Rock, now. Therefore, I ask, who comes to make an end of the Lone Wolf? For it is my right, by the Law of the Jungle, that ye come one by one."

There was a long hush, for no single wolf cared to fight Akela to the death. Then Shere Khan roared: "Bah! What have we to do with this toothless fool? He is doomed to die! It is the man-cub who has lived too long. Free People, he was my meat from the first. Give him to me. I am weary of this man-wolf folly. He has troubled the jungle for ten seasons. Give me the man-cub, or I will hunt here always, and not give you one bone. He is a man, a man's child, and from the marrow of my bones I hate him!"

Then more than half the Pack yelled: "A man! A man! What has a man to do with us? Let him go to his own place."

"And turn all the people of the villages

against us?" clamored Shere Khan. "No, give him to me. He is a man, and none of us can look him between the eyes."

Akela lifted his head again and said, "He has eaten our food. He has slept with us. He has driven game for us. He has broken no word of the Law of the Jungle."

"Also, I paid for him with a bull when he was accepted. The worth of a bull is little, but Bagheera's honor is something that he will perhaps fight for," said Bagheera in his gentlest voice.

"A bull paid ten years ago!" the Pack snarled. "What do we care for bones ten years old?"

"Or for a pledge of honor?" said Bagheera, his white teeth bared under his lip. "Well are ye called the Free People!"

"No man's cub can run with the people of the jungle," howled Shere Khan. "Give him to me!"

"He is our brother in all but blood," Akela went on, "and ye would kill him here! In truth, I have lived too long. Some of ye are eaters of cattle, and I have heard that others, under Shere Khan's teaching, go by dark night and snatch children from the villager's doorstep. Therefore I know ye to be cowards, and it is to those cowards I speak. It is certain that I must die, and my life is of no worth, or I would offer it in the man-cub's place. But for the sake of the Honor of the Pack—a little matter that by being without a leader ye have forgotten—I promise that if ye let the man-cub go to his own place, I will not, when my time comes to die, bare one tooth against ye. I will die without fighting. That will at least save the Pack three lives. I cannot do more; but if ye will agree, I can save ye the shame that comes of killing a brother against whom there is no fault—a brother spoken for and bought into the Pack according to the Law of the Jungle."

"He is a man—a man—a man!" snarled the Pack. And most of the wolves began to gather round Shere Khan, whose tail was beginning to switch.

"Now it's up to you," said Bagheera to Mowgli. "We can do no more except fight."

Mowgli stood upright—the fire-pot in his hands. Then he stretched out his arms, and yawned in the face of the Council; but he was furious with rage and sorrow, for the wolves had never told him how they hated him. "Listen you!" he cried. "There is no need for this jabber. Ye have told me so often tonight that I am a man (and indeed I would have been a wolf with you to my life's end) that I feel your words are true. So I will not call ye my brothers any more. What ye will do, and what ye will not do, is not yours to say. That matter is with me; and that we may see the matter more plainly, I, the man, have brought here a little of the Red Flower which ye fear."

He flung the fire pot on the ground, and some of the red coals lit a tuft of dried moss that flared up, as all the Council drew back in terror before the leaping flames.

Mowgli thrust his dead branch into the fire till the twigs lit and crackled, and whirled it above his head among the cowering wolves.

"Thou art the master," whispered Bagheera. "Save Akela from the death. He was ever thy friend."

Akela, the grim old wolf who had never asked for mercy in his life, gave one pitiful look at Mowgli as the boy stood all naked, his long black hair tossing over his shoulders in the light of the blazing branch that made the shadows jump and quiver.

"Good!" said Mowgli, staring round slowly. "I see that ye are afraid. I go from you to my own people—if they are my own people. The jungle is shut to me, and I must forget your talk and your companionship. But I will be more merciful than ye are. Because I was your brother in all but blood, I promise that when I am a man among men I will not betray ye to men as ye have betrayed me." He kicked the fire with his foot, and the sparks flew up. "There shall be no war between any of us in the Pack. But there is a debt to pay before I go." He strode forward to where Shere Khan sat blinking stupidly at the flames, and caught him by the tuft on his chin. Bagheera followed in case of accidents. "Up!" Mowgli cried. "Up, when a man speaks, or I will set that coat ablaze!"

Shere Khan's ears lay flat back on his head, and he shut his eyes, for the blazing branch was very near.

"This cattle-killer said he would kill me in the Council because he had not killed me when I was a cub. Move just one whisker, Lungri, and I will ram the Red Flower down thy throat!" He beat Shere Khan over the head with the branch, and the tiger whimpered and whined in an agony of fear.

"Pah! Singed jungle cat—go now! But remember when I next come to the Council Rock, as a man should come, it will be with Shere Khan's hide on my head. Now let Akela go free to live as he pleases. Ye will not kill him, because that is not my will. Nor do I think that ye will sit here any longer, lolling out your tongues as though ye were somebodies! Go!" The fire was burning furiously at the end of the branch, and Mowgli struck right and left round the circle, and the wolves ran howling with the sparks burning their fur. At last there were only Akela, Bagheera, and perhaps ten wolves that had taken Mowgli's side. Then something began to hurt Mowgli inside him, as he had never been hurt in his life before, and he caught his breath and sobbed, and the tears ran down his face.

"What is it? What is it?" he said. "I do not wish to leave the jungle, and I do not know what this is. Am I dying, Bagheera?"

"No, Little Brother. They are only tears such as men use," said Bagheera. "Now I know thou art a man, and a man's cub no longer. The jungle is indeed shut to thee from now on. Let them fall, Mowgli. They are only tears." Mowgli had never cried in all his life before. Now he sat and cried as though his heart would break.

"Now," he said, "I will go to men. But first I must say farewell to my mother." He went to the cave where she lived with Father Wolf, and he cried on her coat, while the four cubs howled miserably.

"Ye will not forget me?" said Mowgli.

"Never while we can follow a trail," said the cubs. "Come to the foot of the hill when thou art a man, and we will talk to thee; and we will come into the croplands to play with thee by night."

"Come soon!" said Father Wolf. "Oh, wise little frog, come again soon; for we are old, thy mother and I."

"Come soon," said Mother Wolf, "little naked son of mine. For, listen, child of man, I loved thee more than ever I loved my cubs."

"I will surely come," said Mowgli. "And when I come it will be to lay out Shere Khan's hide upon the Council Rock. Do not forget me! Tell them in the jungle never to forget me!"

The dawn was beginning to break when Mowgli went down the hillside alone, to meet those mysterious things that are called men.

CHAPTER 2

All that is told here happened some time before Mowgli was turned away from the Seeonee Wolf Pack, or took revenge on Shere Khan the tiger. It was in the days when Baloo was teaching him the Law of the Jungle. The big, serious, old brown bear was delighted to have so quick a pupil, for the young wolves will only learn as much of the Law of the Jungle as applies to their own pack and tribe, and run away as soon as they can repeat the Hunting Verse—"Feet that make no noise; eyes that can see in the dark; ears that can hear the winds in their lairs; and sharp white teeth;

37

all these things are the marks of our brothers except Tabaqui the Jackal and the Hyena whom we hate." But Mowgli, as a man-cub, had to learn a great deal more than this. Sometimes Bagheera the Black Panther would come lounging through the jungle to see how his pet was getting on, and would purr with his head against a tree while Mowgli recited the day's lesson to Baloo.

The boy could climb almost as well as he could swim, and swim almost as well as he could run. So Baloo, the Teacher of the Law, taught him the Wood and Water Laws: how to tell a rotten branch from a sound one; how to speak politely to the wild bees when he came upon a hive of them fifty feet above ground; what to say to Mang the Bat when he disturbed him in the branches at midday; and how to warn the water-snakes in the pools before he splashed down among them. None of the Jungle People like being disturbed— all are very ready to fly at an intruder. Then, too, Mowgli was taught the Strangers' Hunting Call, which must be repeated aloud till it is answered, whenever one of the Jungle People hunts outside his own grounds. It means, translated, "Give me leave to hunt here because I am hungry." And the answer is,

"Hunt then for food, but not for pleasure."

All this shows you how much Mowgli had to learn by heart, and he grew very tired of saying the same thing over a hundred times. But, as Baloo said to Bagheera, one day when Mowgli had been smacked and had run off in a temper, "A man's cub is a man's cub, and he must learn all the Law of the Jungle."

"But think how small he is," said the Black Panther, who would have spoiled Mowgli if he had had his own way. "How can his little head carry all thy long talk?"

"Is there anything in the jungle too little

to be killed? No. That is why I teach him these things, and that is why I hit him, very softly, when he forgets."

"Softly! What does thou know of softness, old Iron-feet?" Bagheera grunted. "His face is all bruised today by thy—softness. *Ugh.*"

"Better that he should be bruised from head to foot by one who loves him than he should come to harm through ignorance," Baloo answered very earnestly. "I am now teaching him the Master Words of the Jungle that shall protect him from the birds and the Snake People, and all that hunt on four feet, except his own pack. He will now be protected from all the jungle, if he will only remember the words. Is that not worth a little beating?"

"Well, be careful then that thou does not kill the man-cub. He is no tree trunk to sharpen thy blunt claws upon. And what are those Master Words? Though I am more likely to give help than to ask it"—Bagheera stretched out one paw and admired the steel-blue, ripping-chisel talons at the end of it—"still I should like to know."

"I will call Mowgli and he shall say them—if he will. Come, Little Brother!"

"My head is ringing like a bee tree," said a sullen little voice over their heads, and

Mowgli slid down a tree trunk very angry and indignant, adding as he reached the ground: "I come for Bagheera and not for thee, fat old Baloo!"

"That is all right with me," said Baloo, though he was hurt and grieved. "Tell Bagheera, then, the Master Words of the Jungle that I have taught thee this day."

"Master Words for which people?" said Mowgli, delighted to show off. "The jungle has many tongues. I know them all."

"A little thou knowest, but not much. See, O Bagheera, they never thank their teacher. Not one small wolfling has ever come back to thank old Baloo for his teachings. Say the word for the Hunting-People, then, great scholar."

"We be of one blood, ye and I," said Mowgli, giving the words the Bear accent which all the Hunting People use.

"Good. Now for the birds."

Mowgli repeated, with the Bird's whistle at the end of the sentence.

"Now for the Snake-People," said Bagheera.

The answer was a perfectly indescribable hiss, and Mowgli kicked up his feet behind, clapped his hands together to applaud himself, and jumped onto Bagheera's back, where he sat sideways, drumming with his heels on the glossy skin and making the worst faces he could think of at Baloo.

"There—there! That was worth a little bruise," said the brown bear tenderly. "Some day thou will remember me." Then he turned aside to tell Bagheera how he had begged the Master Words from Hathi the Wild Elephant, who knows all about these things, and how Hathi had taken Mowgli down to a pool to get the Snake Word from a water-snake, because Baloo could not pronounce it, and how Mowgli was now reasonably safe against all accidents in the jungle, because neither snake nor bird nor beast would hurt him.

"No one then is to be feared," Baloo concluded, patting his big furry stomach with pride.

"Except his own tribe," said Bagheera, under his breath; and then aloud to Mowgli, "Be careful of my ribs, Little Brother! What is all this dancing up and down?"

Mowgli had been trying to make himself heard by pulling at Bagheera's shoulder fur and kicking hard. When the two listened to him, he was shouting at the top of his voice, "And so I shall have a tribe of my own, and lead them through the branches all day long."

"What is this new folly, little dreamer of dreams?" said Bagheera.

"Yes, and throw branches and dirt at old Baloo," Mowgli went on. "They have promised me this. Ah!"

"*Whoof!*" Baloo's big paw scooped Mowgli off Bagheera's back, and as the boy lay between the big forepaws, he could see the Bear was angry.

"Mowgli," said Baloo, "thou has been talking with the Bandar-log—the Monkey People."

Mowgli looked at Bagheera to see if the Panther was angry too, and Bagheera's eyes were as hard as jade stones.

"Thou hast been with the Monkey People—the gray apes—the people without a law—the eaters of everything. That is a great shame."

"When Baloo hurt my head," said Mowgli (he was still on his back), "I went away, and the gray apes came down from the trees and had pity on me. No one else cared." He sniffled a little.

"The pity of the Monkey People!" Baloo snorted. "The stillness of the mountain stream! The cool of the summer sun! And then what, man-cub?"

"And then, and then, they gave me nuts and pleasant things to eat, and they—they carried me in their arms up to the top of the trees and said I was their blood brother except that I had no tail, and that I should be their leader some day."

"They have *no* leader," said Bagheera. "They lie. They have always lied."

"They were very kind and asked me to come again. Why have I never been taken among the Monkey People? They stand on their feet as I do. They do not hit me with their hard paws. They play all day. Let me get up! Bad Baloo, let me up! I will play with them again."

"Listen, man-cub," said the Bear, his voice rumbling like thunder on a hot night. "I have taught thee all the Law of the Jungle for all the peoples of the jungle—except the Monkey-Folk who live in the trees. They have no law. They are outcasts. They have no speech of their own, but use stolen words which they overhear when they listen, waiting up above in the branches. Their way is not our way. They are without leaders. They have no memory. They boast and chatter and pretend that they are a great people about to do great things in the jungle, but the falling of a nut turns their minds to laughter, and all is forgotten. We of the jungle have no dealings with them. We do not drink where the monkeys drink; we do not go where the monkeys go; we do not hunt where they hunt; we do not die where they die. Has thou ever heard me speak of the Bandar-log till today?"

"No," said Mowgli in a whisper, for the forest was very still now that Baloo had finished.

"The Jungle-People do not speak of them or think about them. There are many of them, and they are evil, dirty, shameless; and they desire, if they even have any fixed desire, to be noticed by the Jungle People. But we do not notice them even when they throw nuts and filth on our heads."

He had hardly spoken when a shower of nuts and twigs spattered down through the branches. They could hear coughing and howling and angry jumping high up in the air among the thin branches.

"The Monkey-People are forbidden," said Baloo, "forbidden to the Jungle-People. Remember."

"Forbidden," said Bagheera, "but I still think Baloo should have warned thee against them."

"I—I? How was I to guess he would play with such dirt. The Monkey People! *Faugh!*"

A fresh shower came down on their heads, and the two trotted away, taking Mowgli with them. What Baloo had said about the monkeys was perfectly true. They belonged to the tree-tops, and as beasts very seldom look up, there was no occasion for the monkeys and the Jungle-People to cross each other's path. But whenever they found a sick wolf, or a wounded tiger or bear, the monkeys would torment him, and would throw sticks and nuts at any beast for fun and in the hope of being noticed. Then they would howl and shriek senseless songs and invite the Jungle-People to climb up their trees and fight them. They would start furious battles over nothing among themselves, and leave the dead monkeys where the Jungle-People could see them. They were always just about to have a leader, and laws and customs of their own, but they never did, because their memories would not hold over from day to day, and so they explained things by making up a saying, "What the Bandar-log think now the jungle will think later," and that comforted them a great deal. None of the beasts could reach them, but on the other hand none of the beasts would notice them, and that was why they were so pleased when Mowgli came to play with them, and they heard how angry Baloo was.

They never meant to do any more—the Bandar-log never mean anything at all; but one of them invented what seemed to him a brilliant idea. He told all the others that Mowgli would be a useful person to keep in the tribe, because he could weave sticks together for protection from the wind; so, if they caught him, they could make him teach them. Of course Mowgli, as a woodcutter's child, had inherited all sorts of instincts, and used to make little huts of fallen branches without even thinking how he came to do it. The Monkey People, watching in the trees, considered his play most wonderful. This time, they said, they were really going to have a leader and become the wisest people in the jungle—so wise that everyone else would notice and envy them. So they followed Baloo and Bagheera and Mowgli through the jungle very quietly till it was time for the midday nap, and Mowgli, who was very much ashamed of himself, slept between the Panther and the Bear, resolving to have no more to do with the Monkey People.

The next thing he remembered was feeling hands on his legs and arms—hard, strong, little hands—and then a swash of branches in his face, and then he was staring down through the swaying boughs as Baloo woke the jungle with his deep cries and Bagheera bounded up the trunk with every tooth bared. The Bandar-log howled with triumph and scuffled away to the upper branches where Bagheera dared not follow, shouting: "He has noticed us! Bagheera has noticed us. All the Jungle People admire us for our skill and our cunning." Then they began their flight; and the flight of the Monkey-People through tree-land is one of the things nobody can describe.

They have their regular roads and cross-roads, up hills and down hills, all laid out from fifty to seventy or a hundred feet above ground, and by these they can travel even at night if necessary. Two of the strongest monkeys caught Mowgli under their arms and swung off with him through the treetops, twenty feet at a bound. Had they been alone, they could have gone twice as fast, but the boy's weight held them back. Sick and giddy as Mowgli was, he could not help enjoying the wild rush, though the glimpses of earth

far down below frightened him, and the terrible jerking back and forth at the end of the swing over nothing but empty air brought his heart into his throat. His captors would rush him up a tree till he felt the thinnest topmost branches crackle and bend under them, and then with a cough and a whoop would fling themselves into the air outward and downward, and swing up, hanging by their hands or their feet to the lower limbs of the next tree. Sometimes he could see for miles and miles across the still green jungle, as a man on the top of a mast can see for miles across the sea. Then the branches and leaves would lash him across the face, and he and his two guards would be almost down to earth again. So, bounding and crashing and whooping and yelling, the whole tribe of Bandar-log swept along the tree-roads with Mowgli as their prisoner.

For a time he was afraid of being dropped. Then he grew angry, but knew better than to struggle, and then he began to think. The first thing to do was to send back word to Baloo and Bagheera, for at the pace the monkeys were going, he knew his friends would be left far behind. It was useless to look down, for he could only see the top of the branches, so he stared upward and saw Chil the Bird, far away in the blue, balancing and wheeling as he kept watch over the jungle waiting for things to die. Chil saw that the monkeys were carrying something, and dropped a few hundred yards to find out whether their load was good to eat. He whistled with surprise when he saw Mowgli being dragged up to a treetop and heard him give the Bird call—"We be of one blood, thou and I." The waves of the branches closed over the boy, but Chil flew away to the next tree in time to see the little brown face come up again. "Mark my trail!" Mowgli shouted. "Tell Baloo of the Seeonee Pack and Bagheera of the Council Rock."

"In whose name, Brother?" Chil had never seen Mowgli before, though of course he had heard of him.

"Mowgli, the Frog. Man-cub they call me! Mark my tra-il!"

The last words were shrieked as he was being swung through the air, but Chil nodded and rose up till he looked no bigger than a speck of dust. There he hung, watching the swaying of the treetops with his telescope eyes as Mowgli's escort whirled along.

"They never go far," he said with a chuckle. "They never do what they set out to do.

The Bandar-log are always pecking at new things. This time, if I have any eyesight, they have pecked down trouble for themselves, for Baloo is wise and experienced and Bagheera can, as I know, kill more than goats."

So he rocked on his wings, his feet gathered up under him, and waited.

Meantime, Baloo and Bagheera were furious with rage and grief. Bagheera climbed as he had never climbed before, but the thin branches broke beneath his weight, and he slipped down, his claws full of bark.

"Why did thou not warn the man-cub?" he roared to poor Baloo, who had set off at a clumsy trot in the hope of overtaking the monkeys. "What was the use of half slaying him with blows if thou did not warn him?"

"Hurry! O hurry! We—we may catch them yet!" Baloo panted.

"At that speed? We would not tire a wounded cow. Teacher of the Law—cub-beater—a mile of that rolling to and fro will wear you out. Sit still and think! Make a plan. This is no time for chasing. They may drop him if we follow too close."

"*Arrula! Whoo!* They may have dropped him already, being tired of carrying him. Who can trust the Bandar-log? Put dead bats on my head! Give me black bones to eat! Roll me into the hives of the wild bees that I may be stung to death, and bury me with the Hyena, for I am most miserable of bears! *Arulala! Wahooa!* O Mowgli, Mowgli! Why did I not warn thee against the Monkey-Folk instead of hitting thy head? Perhaps I may have knocked the day's lesson out of his mind, and he will be alone in the jungle without the Master Words."

Baloo clasped his paws over his ears and rolled to and fro moaning.

"At least he recited all the Words correctly a little while ago," said Bagheera impatiently. "Baloo, thou hast neither memory or respect. What would the jungle think if I, the Black Panther, curled myself up like Sahi the Porcupine, and howled?"

"What do I care what the jungle thinks? He may be dead by now."

"Unless and until they drop him from the branches in sport, or kill him out of idleness, I have no fear for the man-cub. He is wise and well taught, and above all he has the eyes that make the Jungle-People afraid. But he is under the evil power of the Bandar-log, and because they live in trees, they have no fear of any of our people." Bagheera licked one forepaw thoughtfully.

"Fool that I am! Oh, fat, brown, root-digging fool that I am," said Baloo, uncoiling himself with a jerk, "it is true what Hathi the Wild Elephant says: *'To each his own fear'*; and they, the Bandar-log, fear Kaa the Rock Snake. He can climb as well as they can. He steals the young monkeys in the night. The whisper of his name makes their wicked tails cold. Let us go to Kaa."

"What will he do for us? He is not of our tribe, being footless—and with the most evil eyes," said Bagheera.

"He is very old and very cunning. Above all, he is always hungry," said Baloo hopefully. "Promise him many goats."

"He sleeps for a full month after he has once eaten. He may be asleep now, and even if he were awake, what if he would rather kill his own goats?" Bagheera, who did not know much about Kaa, was naturally suspicious.

"Then in that case, thou and I together, old hunter, might make him see reason." Here Baloo rubbed his faded brown shoulder against the Panther, and they went off to look for Kaa the Rock Python.

They found him stretched out on a warm ledge in the afternoon sun, admiring his beautiful new coat, for he had been in retirement for the last ten days changing his skin, and now he was very splendid—darting his big blunt-nosed head along the ground, and twisting the thirty feet of his body into fantastic knots and curves, and licking his lips as he thought of his dinner to come.

"He has not eaten," said Baloo, with a grunt of relief, as soon as he saw the beautifully mottled brown and yellow jacket. "Be careful, Bagheera! He is always a little blind after he has changed his skin, and very quick to strike."

Kaa was not a poisonous snake—in fact he rather despised the poisonous snakes as cowards. His strength lay in his hug, and when he had wrapped his huge coils around anybody, there was no more to be said. "Good hunting!" cried Baloo, sitting up on his haunches. Like all snakes of his breed, Kaa was rather deaf, and did not hear the call at first. Then he curled up ready for attack, his head lowered.

"Good hunting for us all," Kaa answered. "Oho, Baloo, what dost thou do here? Good hunting, Bagheera. At least one of us needs food. Is there any news of game afoot? A doe now, or even a young buck? I am as empty as a dried well."

"We are hunting," said Baloo carelessly. He knew that you must not hurry Kaa. He is too big.

"Give me permission to come with you," said Kaa. "A blow more or less is nothing to thee, Bagheera or Baloo, but I—I have to wait and wait for days in a wood-path and climb half a night on the mere chance of catching a young ape. *Psshaw!* The branches are not what they were when I was young. They are all rotten twigs and dry boughs."

"Maybe thy great weight has something to do with the problem," said Baloo.

"I am a fair length—a fair length," said Kaa with a little pride. "But for all that, it is the fault of this new-grown timber. I came very near to falling on my last hunt—very near indeed—and the noise of my slipping, for my tail was not tight wrapped around the tree, awakened the Bandar-log, and they called me most evil names."

"Footless, yellow earth-worm," said Bagheera under his whiskers, as though he were trying to remember something.

"*Sssss!* Have they ever called me that?" said Kaa.

"It was something of that kind that they shouted to us last moon, but we never noticed them. They will say anything—even that thou hast lost all thy teeth, and will not face anything bigger than a kid, because (they are indeed shameless, these Bandar-log)—because thou art afraid of the he-goat's horns," Bagheera went on sweetly.

Now a snake, especially a wary old python like Kaa, very seldom shows that he is angry, but Baloo and Bagheera could see the big swallowing muscles on either side of Kaa's throat ripple and bulge.

"The Bandar-log have shifted their grounds," he said quietly. "When I came up into the sun today I heard them whooping among the tree-tops."

"It—it is the Bandar-log that we follow now," said Baloo, but the words stuck in his throat, for that was the first time in his memory that one of the Jungle-People had admitted to being interested in the doings of the monkeys.

"Beyond doubt then it is no small thing that takes two such hunters—leaders in their own jungle I am certain—on the trail of the Bandar-log," Kaa replied courteously, as he swelled with curiosity.

"Indeed," Baloo began, "I am no more than the old and sometimes very foolish Teacher of the Law to the Seeonee wolf-cubs, and Bagheera here—"

"Is Bagheera," said the Black Panther, and his jaws shut with a snap, for he did not believe in being humble. "The trouble is this, Kaa. Those nut-stealers and pickers of palm leaves have stolen away our man-cub of whom thou hast perhaps heard."

"I heard some news from Sahi (his quills make him presumptuous) of a man-thing that was entered into a wolf pack, but I did not believe it. Sahi is full of stories half heard and very badly told."

"But it is true. He is such a man-cub as never was," said Baloo. "The best and wisest and boldest of man-cubs—my own pupil, who shall make the name of Baloo famous through all the jungles; and besides, I—we—love him, Kaa."

"*Ts! Ts!*" said Kaa, weaving his head to and fro. "I also have known what love is. There are tales I could tell that—"

"That need a clear night when we are all well fed to praise properly," said Bagheera quickly. "Our man-cub is in the hands of the Bandar-log now, and we know that of all the Jungle-People they fear Kaa alone."

"They fear me alone. They have good reason," said Kaa. "Chattering, foolish, vain—vain, foolish, and chattering, are the monkeys. But a man-thing in their hands is an unlucky situation. They grow tired of the nuts they pick, and throw them down. They carry a branch half a day, meaning to do great things with it, and then they snap it in two. That man-thing is not to be envied. They called me also—'yellow fish' was it not?"

"Worm—worm—earth-worm,"   said Bagheera, "as well as other things which I cannot now say for shame."

"We must remind them to speak well of their master. *Aaa-ssp!* We must help their wandering memories. Now, where did they go with the cub?"

"The jungle alone knows. Toward the sunset, I believe," said Baloo. "We had thought that thou would know, Kaa."

"I? How? I take them when they come in my way, but I do not hunt the Bandar-log, or frogs—or green scum on a water-hole, for that matter."

"Up, Up! Up, Up! *Hillo! Illo! Illo*, look up, Baloo of the Seeonee Wolf Pack!"

Baloo looked up to see where the voice came from, and there was Chil the Bird, sweeping down with the sun shining on the upturned wings. It was near Chil's bedtime, but he had flown all over the jungle looking for the Bear and had missed him in the thick foliage.

"What is it?" said Baloo.

"I have seen Mowgli among the Bandar-log. He asked me to tell you. I watched. The Bandar-log have taken him beyond the river to the monkey city—to the Cold Lairs. They may stay there for a night, or ten nights, or an hour. I have told the bats to watch through the dark time. That is my message. Good hunting, all you below!"

"Full gorge and a deep sleep to you, Chil," cried Bagheera. "I will remember thee in my next kill, and put aside the head for thee alone, O best of birds!"

"It is nothing. It is nothing. The boy knew the Master Word. I could have done no less," and Chil circled up again to his roost.

"He has not forgotten to use his tongue," said Baloo with a chuckle of pride. "To think of one so young remembering the Master Word for the birds too while he was being pulled across trees!"

"It was most firmly driven into him," said
Bagheera. "But I am proud of him, and now
we must go to the Cold Lairs."

They all knew where that place was, but
few of the Jungle People ever went there.
What they called the Cold Lairs was an old
deserted city, lost and buried in the jungle,
and beasts seldom use a place that men have
once used. The wild boar will, but the hunting tribes do not. Besides, the monkeys lived
there as much as they could be said to live
anywhere, so no self-respecting animal would
come within eyeshot of it except in times of
drought, when the half-ruined tanks and
reservoirs held a little water.

"It is half a night's journey—at full
speed," said Bagheera. Baloo looked very serious. "I will go as fast as I can," he said anxiously.

"We dare not wait for thee. Follow, Baloo.
We must go quickly—Kaa and I."

"Feet or no feet, I can keep up with all thy
four," said Kaa shortly. Baloo made one effort
to hurry, but had to sit down panting, and so
they left him to come along later, while
Bagheera hurried forward, at the quick pan-
ther-pace. Kaa said nothing, but, strive as

Bagheera might, the huge Rock-python kept up with him. When they came to a stream, Bagheera moved ahead, because he bounded across while Kaa swam, his head and two feet of his neck clearing the water. But on level ground Kaa made up the distance.

"By the Broken Lock that freed me," said Bagheera, when twilight had fallen, "thou art no slow goer!"

"I am hungry," said Kaa. "Besides, they called me speckled frog."

"Worm—earth-worm, and yellow to boot."

"All the same. Let us go on," and Kaa seemed to pour himself along the ground, finding the shortest road with his steady eyes, and keeping to it.

In the Cold Lairs, the Monkey-People were not thinking of Mowgli's friends at all. They had brought the boy to the Lost City, and were very much pleased with themselves for the moment. Mowgli had never seen an Indian city before, and though this was almost a heap of ruins, to him it seemed very wonderful and splendid. Some king had built it long ago on a little hill. You could still trace the stone causeways that led up to the ruined gates where the last splinters of wood clung to the worn, rusted hinges. Trees had grown into and out of the walls; the battle towers were tumbled down and decayed, and wild ivy hung out of the windows of the towers on the walls in bushy hanging clumps.

A great roofless palace crowned the hill, and the marble of the courtyards and the fountains was split and stained with red and green. The very cobblestones in the courtyard where the king's elephants used to live had been uprooted and torn apart by grasses and young trees. From the palace you could see the rows and rows of roofless houses that made up the city looking like empty honeycombs filled with blackness; the shapeless block of stone that had been an idol in the square where four roads met; the pits at street corners where the public wells once stood; and the shattered domes of temples with wild figs sprouting on their sides. The monkeys called the place their city and pretended to despise the Jungle-People because they lived in the forest. And yet they never knew what the buildings were made for or how to use them. They would sit in circles in the hall of the king's council chamber and scratch for fleas and pretend to be men. Or they would run in and out of the roofless houses and collect pieces of plaster and old bricks in a corner and then forget where they had hidden them. They would fight and cry in scuffling crowds and then break off to play up and down the terraces of the king's garden, where they would shake the rose trees and the oranges in sport to see the fruit and flowers fall. They explored all the passages and dark tunnels in the palace and the hundreds of little dark rooms, but they never remembered what they had seen and what they had not. And so they drifted about in ones and twos or crowds, telling each other that they were doing as men did. They drank at the tanks and made the water all muddy, and then they fought over it. Then they would all rush together in mobs and shout: "There is no one in the jungle so wise and good and clever and strong and gentle as the Bandar-log." Then all would begin again till they grew tired of the city and went back to the treetops, hoping the Jungle-People would notice them.

Mowgli, who had been trained under the Law of the Jungle, did not like or understand this kind of life. The monkeys dragged him into the Cold Lairs late in the afternoon, and instead of going to sleep, as Mowgli would have done after a long journey, they joined hands and danced about and sang their foolish songs. One of the monkeys made a speech and told his companions that Mowgli's capture marked a new thing in the history of the Bandar-log, for Mowgli was going to show them how to weave sticks and canes together as a protection against rain and cold. Mowgli picked up some vines and began to work them in and out, and the monkeys tried to imitate;

but in a very few minutes they lost interest and began to pull their friends' tails or jump up and down on all fours, coughing.

"I wish to eat," said Mowgli. "I am a stranger in this part of the jungle. Bring me food, or give me leave to hunt here."

Twenty or thirty monkeys bounded away to bring him nuts and wild pawpaws. But they ended up fighting on the road, and it was too much trouble to go back with what was left of the fruit. Mowgli was sore and angry as well as hungry, and he roamed through the empty city giving the Strangers' Hunting Call from time to time, but no one answered him. Mowgli felt that he had reached a very bad place indeed. "All that Baloo has said about the Bandar-log is true," he thought to himself. "They have no Law, no Hunting Call, and no leaders—nothing but foolish words and little picking thievish hands. So if I am starved or killed here, it will be all my own fault. But I must try to return to my own jungle. Baloo will surely beat me, but that is better than chasing silly rose leaves with the Bandar-log."

No sooner had he walked to the city wall than the monkeys pulled him back, telling him that he did not know how happy he was, and pinching him to make him grateful. He set his teeth and said nothing, but went with the shouting monkeys to a terrace above the red sandstone reservoirs that were half-full of rain water. There was a ruined summer house of white marble in the center of the terrace, built for queens dead a hundred years ago. The domed roof had half fallen in and blocked up the underground passage from the palace by which the queens used to enter. But the walls were made of screens of beautiful, milk-white marble cut like lace—set with agates and carnelian and jasper and lapis lazuli. As the moon came up behind the hill, it shone through the open work, casting shadows on the ground like black velvet embroidery. Sore, sleepy, and hungry as he was, Mowgli could not help laughing when the Bandar-log began, twenty at a time, to tell him how great and wise and strong and gentle they were, and how foolish he was to wish to leave them. "We are great. We are free. We are wonderful. We are the most wonderful people in all the jungle! We all say so, and so it must be true," they shouted. "Now as you are a new listener and can carry our words back to the Jungle-People so that they may notice us in future, we will tell you all about our most excellent selves."

Mowgli made no objection, so the monkeys

gathered by hundreds and hundreds on the terrace to listen to their own speakers singing the praises of the Bandar-log. And whenever a speaker stopped for want of breath, they would all shout together: "This is true; we all say so." Mowgli nodded and blinked and said "Yes" when they asked him a question. His head spun with the noise. "Tabaqui the Jackal must have bitten all these people," he said to himself, "and now they have madness. Certainly this is *dewanee*, the madness. Do they never go to sleep? Now there is a cloud coming to cover the moon. If it were only a big enough cloud, I might try to run away in the darkness. But I am tired."

That same cloud was being watched by his two good friends in the ruined ditch below the city wall, for Bagheera and Kaa, knowing well how dangerous the Monkey-People were in large numbers, did not wish to run any risks. The monkeys never fight unless they are a hundred to one, and few in the jungle care for those odds.

"I will go to the west wall," Kaa whispered, "and come down swiftly with the slope of the ground in my favor. They will not throw themselves upon my back in their hundreds, but—"

"I know it," said Bagheera. "Would that Baloo were here, but we must do what we can. When that cloud covers the moon, I shall go to the terrace. They hold some sort of council there over the boy."

"Good hunting," said Kaa grimly, and glided away to the west wall. The west wall happened to be the least ruined of any, and the big snake was delayed awhile before he could find a way up the stones. The cloud hid the moon, and as Mowgli wondered what would come next, he heard Bagheera's light feet on the terrace. The Black Panther had raced up the slope almost without a sound and was striking—he knew better than to waste time in biting—right and left among the monkeys, who were seated round Mowgli in circles fifty and sixty deep. There was a howl of fright and rage, and then as Bagheera tripped on the rolling kicking bodies beneath him, a monkey shouted: "There is only one here! Kill him! Kill."

A scuffling mass of monkeys, biting, scratching, tearing, and pulling, closed over Bagheera, while five or six took hold of Mowgli, dragged him up the wall of the summerhouse and pushed him through the hole of the broken dome. A man-trained boy would have been badly bruised, for the fall was a good fifteen feet, but Mowgli fell as Baloo had taught him to fall and landed on his feet.

"Stay there," shouted the monkeys, "till we have killed thy friends, and later we will play with thee—if the Poison-People leave thee alive."

"We be of one blood, ye and I," said Mowgli, quickly giving the Snake's Call. He could hear rustling and hissing in the rubbish all round him and gave the Call a second time, to make sure.

"Even ssso! Down hoods all!" said half a dozen low voices (every ruin in India sooner or later becomes a dwelling place of snakes, and the old summerhouse was alive with cobras). "Stand still, Little Brother, for the sound of thy feet may do us harm."

Mowgli stood as quietly as he could, peering through the open work and listening to the furious din of the fight round the Black Panther—the yells and chattering and scuffling, and Bagheera's deep, hoarse cough as he backed and bucked and twisted and plunged under the heaps of his enemies. For the first time since he was born, Bagheera was fighting for his life.

"Baloo must be at hand; Bagheera would

not have come alone," Mowgli thought. And then he called aloud: "To the tank, Bagheera. Roll to the water tanks. Roll and plunge! Get to the water!"

Bagheera heard, and the cry that told him Mowgli was safe gave him new courage. He worked his way desperately, inch by inch, straight for the reservoirs, halting in silence. Then from the ruined wall nearest the jungle rose up the rumbling war-shout of Baloo. The old Bear had done his best, but he could not come before. "Bagheera," he shouted, "I am here. I climb! I hurry! *Ahuwora!* The stones slip under my feet! Wait, I am coming, O most infamous Bandar-log!" He panted up the terrace only to disappear, covered up to his head in a wave of monkeys. But he threw himself squarely on his haunches, and, spreading out his forepaws, hugged as many as he could hold, and then began to hit with a regular *bat-bat-bat*, like the flipping strokes of a paddle wheel. A crash and a splash told Mowgli that Bagheera had fought his way to the tank where the monkeys could not follow. The Panther lay gasping for breath, his head just out of the water, while the monkeys stood three deep on the red steps, dancing up and down with rage, ready to spring upon him from all sides if he came out to help Baloo. It was then that Bagheera lifted up his dripping chin, and in despair gave the Snake's Call for protection—"We be of one blood, ye and I"—for he believed that Kaa had turned and left at the last minute. Even Baloo, half smothered under the monkeys on the edge of the terrace, could not help chuckling as he heard the Black Panther asking for help.

Kaa had only just worked his way over the west wall, landing with a crash that dislodged a stone into the ditch. He had no intention of losing any advantage of the ground, and coiled and uncoiled himself once or twice, to be sure that every foot of his long body was in working order. All that while the fight with Baloo went on, and the monkeys yelled in the tank around Bagheera, and Mang the Bat, flying to and fro, carried the news of the great battle over the jungle, till even Hathi the Wild Elephant trumpeted. And far away, scattered bands of the Monkey-Folk woke and came leaping along the tree-roads to help their comrades in the Cold Lairs. And the noise of the fight roused all the day birds for miles round. Then Kaa came straight, quickly, and anxious to kill. The fighting strength of a python is in the driving blow of his head backed by all the strength and weight of his body. If you can imagine a lance, or a battering ram, or a hammer weighing nearly half a ton driven by a cool, quiet mind living in the handle of it, you can roughly imagine what Kaa was like when he fought. A python four or five feet long can knock a man down if he hits him squarely in the chest, and Kaa was thirty feet long, as you know. His first stroke was delivered into the heart of the crowd round Baloo. There was no need of a second. The monkeys scattered with cries of—"Kaa! It is Kaa! Run! Run!"

Generations of monkeys had been scared into good behavior by the stories their elders told them of Kaa, the night thief, who could slip along the branches as quietly as moss grows and steal away the strongest monkey that ever lived. There were stories of old Kaa, who could make himself look so like a dead branch or a rotten stump that the wisest were deceived, till the branch caught them. Kaa was everything that the monkeys feared in the jungle, for none of them knew the limits of his power, none of them could look him in the face, and none had ever come alive out of his hug. And so they ran, stammering with terror, to the walls and the roofs of the houses, and

Baloo drew a deep breath of relief. His fur was much thicker than Bagheera's, but he had suffered sorely in the fight. Then Kaa opened his mouth for the first time and spoke one long hissing word, and the far-away monkeys, hurrying to the defense of the Cold Lairs, stayed where they were, cowering, till the loaded branches bent and crackled under them. The monkeys on the walls and the empty houses stopped their cries, and in the stillness that fell upon the city, Mowgli heard Bagheera shaking his wet sides as he came up from the tank. Then the clamor broke out again. The monkeys leaped higher up the walls. They clung around the necks of the big stone idols and shrieked as they skipped along the battle towers, while Mowgli, dancing in the summerhouse, peeked through the screenwork and hooted owl-fashion between his front teeth, to show his derision and contempt.

"Get the man-cub out of that trap; I can do no more," Bagheera gasped. "Let us take the man-cub and go. They may attack again."

"They will not move till I order them. Stay you *sssso!*" Kaa hissed, and the city was silent once more. "I could not get here sooner, Brother, but I think I heard thee call," he said to Bagheera.

"I—I may have cried out in the battle," Bagheera answered. "Baloo, art thou hurt?

"I am not sure that they did not pull me into a hundred little bearlings," said Baloo, gravely shaking one leg after the other. "I am sore. Kaa, we owe thee, I think, our lives—Bagheera and I."

"No matter. Where is the manling?"

"Here, in a trap. I cannot climb out," cried Mowgli. The curve of the broken dome was above his head.

"Take him away. He dances like Mao the Peacock. He will crush our young," said the cobras inside.

"Hah!" said Kaa with a chuckle, "he has friends everywhere, this manling. Stand back, manling. And hide you, O Poison People. I break down the wall."

Kaa looked carefully till he found a discolored crack in the marble screen showing a weak spot. He made two or three light taps with his head to get a sense of the distance, and then lifting up six feet of his body clear of the ground, sent home half a dozen full-power smashing blows, nose-first. The screen-work broke and fell away in a cloud of dust and rubbish, and Mowgli leaped through the opening and flung himself between Baloo and

Bagheera—an arm around each big neck.

"Art thou hurt?" said Baloo, hugging him softly.

"I am sore, hungry, and quite bruised. But, oh, they have handled ye grievously, my Brothers! You are bleeding."

"And so were the others," said Bagheera, licking his lips and looking at the monkey-dead on the terrace and around the tank.

"It is nothing, it is nothing, if thou art safe, oh, my pride of all little frogs!" whimpered Baloo.

"Of that we shall judge later," said Bagheera, in a dry voice that Mowgli did not like at all. "But here is Kaa to whom we owe the battle and thou owes thy life. Thank him according to our customs, Mowgli."

Mowgli turned and saw the great Python's head swaying a foot above his own.

"So this is the manling," said Kaa. "Very soft is his skin, and he is not unlike the Bandar-log. Be careful, manling, that I do not mistake thee for a monkey some twilight when I have newly changed my coat."

"We be one blood, thou and I," Mowgli answered. "I take my life from thee tonight. My kill shall be thy kill if ever thou art hungry, O Kaa."

"All thanks, Little Brother," said Kaa, though his eyes twinkled. "And what may so bold a hunter kill? I ask that I may follow when next he goes to hunt."

"I kill nothing—I am too little—but I drive goats toward those who can use them. When thou art empty, come to me and see if I speak the truth. I have some skill in these"—he held out his hands—"and if ever thou art in a trap, I may pay the debt which I owe to thee, to Bagheera, and to Baloo, here. Good hunting to ye all, my masters."

"Well said," growled Baloo, for Mowgli had returned thanks very prettily. The Python dropped his head lightly for a minute on Mowgli's shoulder. "A brave heart and a courteous tongue," he said. "They shall carry thee far through the jungle, manling. But now go hence quickly with thy friends. Go and sleep, for the moon sets, and what follows it is not well that thou should see."

The moon was sinking behind the hills, and the lines of trembling monkeys huddled together on the walls and battle towers looked like ragged shaky fringes of things. Baloo went down to the tank for a drink, and Bagheera began to put his fur in order, as Kaa glided out into the center of the terrace and brought his jaws together with a ringing snap that drew all the monkeys' eyes upon him.

"The moon sets," he said. "Is there yet light enough to see?"

From the walls came a moan like the wind in the treetops—"We see, O Kaa."

"Good. Now begins the dance—the Dance of the Hunger of Kaa. Sit still and watch."

He turned twice or thrice in a big circle, weaving his head from right to left. Then he began making loops and figures of eight with his body, and soft, oozy triangles that melted into squares and five-sided figures, and coiled mounds, never resting, never hurrying, and never stopping his low humming song. It grew darker and darker, till at last the dragging, shifting coils disappeared, but they could hear the rustle of the scales.

Baloo and Bagheera stood still as stone, growling in their throats, their neck hair bristling, and Mowgli watched and wondered.

"Bandar-log," said the voice of Kaa at last, "can ye stir foot or hand without my order? Speak!"

"Without thy order we cannot stir foot or hand, O Kaa!"

"Good! Come all one pace nearer to me."

The lines of the monkeys swayed forward helplessly, and Baloo and Bagheera took one stiff step forward with them.

"Nearer!" hissed Kaa, and they all moved again.

Mowgli laid his hands on Baloo and Bagheera to get them away, and the two great beasts jumped as though they had been wakened from a dream.

"Keep thy hand on my shoulder," Bagheera whispered. "Keep it there, or I must go back—must go back to Kaa. Aah!"

"It is only old Kaa making circles on the dust," said Mowgli. "Let us go." And the three slipped off through a gap in the walls to the jungle.

"Whoof!" said Baloo, when he stood under the still trees again. "Never again will I make an ally of Kaa," and he shook himself all over.

"He knows more than we," said Bagheera, trembling. "In a little time, had I stayed, I should have walked down his throat—he would have eaten me alive."

"Many will walk by that road before the moon rises again," said Baloo. "He will have good hunting—in his own way."

"But what was the meaning of it all?" said

Mowgli, who did not know anything of a python's powers of fascination. "I saw no more than a big snake making foolish circles till the dark came. And his nose was all sore. Ho! Ho!"

"Mowgli," said Bagheera angrily, "his nose was sore on *thy* account, as my ears and sides and paws, and Baloo's neck and shoulders are bitten on thy account. Neither Baloo nor Bagheera will be able to hunt with pleasure for many days."

"It is nothing," said Baloo; "we have the man-cub again."

"True, but he has cost us heavily in time which might have been spent in good hunting, in wounds, in hair—I am half plucked along my back—and last of all, in honor. For, remember, Mowgli, I, the Black Panther, was forced to call upon Kaa for protection. And Baloo and I were both made to look stupid as little birds by the Hunger Dance. All this, man-cub, came of thy playing with the Bandar-log."

"True, it is true," said Mowgli sorrowfully. "I am an evil man-cub, and my stomach is sad in me."

"*Umph!* What says the Law of the Jungle, Baloo?"

Baloo did not wish to bring Mowgli into any more trouble, but he could not tamper with the Law, so he mumbled: "Sorrow never replaces punishment. But remember, Bagheera, he is very little."

"I will remember. But he has done mischief, and blows must be dealt now. Mowgli, has thou anything to say?"

"Nothing. I did wrong. Baloo and thou are wounded. It is just."

Bagheera gave him half a dozen love-taps from a panther's point of view (they would hardly have waked one of his own cubs), but for a seven-year-old boy they amounted to as severe a beating as you could wish to avoid. When it was all over Mowgli sneezed, and picked himself up without a word.

"Now," said Bagheera, "jump on my back, Little Brother, and we will go home."

One of the beauties of Jungle Law is that punishment settles all scores. There is no nagging afterward.

Mowgli laid his head down on Bagheera's back and slept so deeply that he never waked when he was put down in the home-cave.

CHAPTER 3

Now we must go back to the first tale. When Mowgli left the wolf's cave after the fight with the Pack at the Council Rock, he went down to the plowed lands where the villagers lived. But he would not stop there because it was too near to the jungle, and he knew that he had made at least one bad enemy at the Council. So he hurried on, keeping to the rough road that ran down the valley, and followed it at a steady jog for nearly twenty miles, till he came to a country that he did not know. The valley opened out into a great plain dotted with rocks and divided by ravines. At one end stood a little village, and at the other, the thick jungle came down in a sweep to the grazing-grounds, and stopped there as though it had been cut off with a hoe. All over the plain, cattle and buffaloes were grazing, and when the little boys in charge of the herds saw Mowgli, they shouted and ran away, and the yellow pariah dogs that hang about every Indian village barked. Mowgli walked on, for he was feeling hungry, and when he came to the village gate, he saw the big thorn-bush that was drawn up before the gate at twilight, pushed to one side.

"Umph!" he said, for he had come across more than one such barricade in his night ramblings after things to eat. "So men are afraid of the People of the Jungle here also." He sat down by the gate, and when a man came out, he stood up, opened his mouth, and pointed down it to show that he wanted food. The man stared and ran back up the one street of the village, shouting for the priest. The priest, who was a big, fat man dressed in white, with a red and yellow mark on his forehead, came to the gate, and with him at least a hundred people, who stared and talked and shouted and pointed at Mowgli.

"They have no manners, these Men

Folk," said Mowgli to himself. "Only the gray ape would behave as they do." So he threw back his long hair and frowned at the crowd.

"What is there to be afraid of?" said the priest. "Look at the marks on his arms and legs. They are the bites of wolves. He is but a wolf-child run away from the jungle."

Of course, in playing together, the cubs had often nipped Mowgli harder than they intended, and there were white scars all over his arms and legs. But he would have been the last person in the world to call these bites, for he knew what real biting meant.

"Arre! Arre!" said two or three women together. "To be bitten by wolves, poor child! He is a handsome boy. He has eyes like red fire. By my honor, Messua, he is not unlike thy boy that was taken by the tiger."

"Let me look," said a woman with heavy copper rings on her wrists and ankles. She peered at Mowgli under the palm of her hand. "Indeed he is not. He is thinner, but he has the very look of my boy."

The priest was a clever man, and he knew that Messua was wife to the richest villager in the place. So he looked up at the sky for a minute and said solemnly: "What the jungle has taken, the jungle has restored. Take the boy into thy house, my sister, and do not forget to honor the priest who sees so far into the lives of men."

"By the Bull that bought me," said Mowgli to himself, "all this talking is like another looking-over by the Pack! Well, if I am a man, a man I must become."

The crowd parted as the woman beckoned Mowgli to her hut, where there was a red lacquered bedstand, a great earthen grain chest with funny raised patterns on it, half a dozen copper cooking pots, an image of a Hindu god in a little alcove, and on the wall a real looking glass, such as they sell at the country fairs.

She gave him a long drink of milk and some bread, and then she laid her hand on his head and looked into his eyes. She thought perhaps that he might be her real son come back from the jungle where the tiger had taken him. So she said, "Nathoo, O Nathoo!" Mowgli did not show that he knew the name. "Does thou not remember the day when I gave thee thy new shoes?" She touched his foot, and it was almost as hard as horn. "No," she said sorrowfully, "those feet have never worn shoes, but thou art very like my Nathoo, and thou shall be my son."

Mowgli was uneasy, because he had never been under a roof before. But as he looked at the thatch, he saw that he could tear it out any time if he wanted to get away, and that the window had no fastenings. "What is the good of a man," he said to himself at last, "if he does not understand man's talk? Now I am as silly and dumb as a man would be with us in the jungle. I must speak their talk."

It was not just for fun that while he was with the wolves he had learned to imitate the challenge of bucks in the jungle and the grunt of the little wild pig. So, as soon as Messua pronounced a word, Mowgli would imitate it almost perfectly, and before dark he had learned the names of many things in the hut.

There was some difficulty at bedtime, because Mowgli would not sleep under anything that looked so much like a panther trap as that hut, and when they shut the door he went through the window. "Give him his will," said Messua's husband. "Remember he has never before slept on a bed. If he is indeed sent in the place of our son, he will not run away."

So Mowgli stretched himself in some long, clean grass at the edge of the field, but before he had closed his eyes, a soft gray nose poked him under the chin.

"Phew!" said Gray Brother (he was the eldest of Mother Wolf's cubs). "This is a poor reward for following thee twenty miles. Thou smellest of wood smoke and cattle—altogether like a man already. Wake, Little Brother; I bring news."

"Are all well in the jungle?" said Mowgli, hugging him.

"All except the wolves that were burned with the Red Flower. Now, listen. Shere Khan has gone away to hunt far off till his coat grows again, for he is badly singed. When he returns, he swears that he will kill thee."

"I am not afraid. I have also made a little promise. But news is always good. I am tired tonight—very tired with new things, Gray Brother—but bring me the news always."

"Thou will not forget that thou art a wolf? Men will not make thee forget?" said Gray Brother anxiously.

"Never. I will always remember that I love thee and all in our cave. But also I will always remember that I have been cast out of the Pack."

"And that thou may be cast out of another pack. Men are only men, Little Brother, and their talk is like the talk of frogs in a pond.

When I come down here again, I will wait for thee in the bamboos at the edge of the grazing-ground."

For three months after that night Mowgli hardly ever left the village gate; he was so busy learning the ways and customs of men. First he had to wear a cloth round him, which annoyed him horribly. And then he had to learn about money, which he did not in the least understand, and about plowing, of which he did not see the use. Then the little children in the village made him very angry. Luckily, the Law of the Jungle had taught him to keep his temper, for in the jungle, life and food depend on keeping your temper; but when they made fun of him because he would not play games or fly kites, or because he mispronounced some word, only the knowledge that it was unsportsmanlike to kill little naked cubs kept him from picking them up and breaking them in two.

He did not know his own strength in the least. In the jungle he knew he was weak compared with the beasts, but in the village, people said that he was as strong as a bull.

And Mowgli did not have the faintest idea of the difference that caste makes between man and man. When the potter's donkey slipped in the clay pit, Mowgli hauled it out by the tail, and helped to stack the pots for their journey to the market at Khanhiwara. This was very shocking, for the potter is a low-caste man, and his donkey is worse. When the priest scolded him, Mowgli threatened to put him on the donkey too. And the priest told Messua's husband that Mowgli had better be set to work as soon as possible. The village head-man told Mowgli that he would have to go out with the buffaloes the next day and herd them while they grazed. No one was more pleased than Mowgli; and that night, because he had been appointed a servant of the village, as it were, he went off to join a circle that met every evening on a masonry platform under a great fig-tree. It was the village club, and the head-man and the watchman and the barber, who knew all the gossip of the village, and old Buldeo, the village hunter, who had a Tower musket, met and smoked. The monkeys sat and talked in the upper branches, and there was a hole under the platform where a cobra lived, and he had his little platter of milk every night because he was sacred. The old men sat around the tree and talked and puffed on the big *huqas* (the water-pipes) till far into the night. They told wonderful tales of gods and men and ghosts. And Buldeo told even more wonderful ones of the ways of beasts in the jungle, till the eyes of the children sitting outside the circle bulged out of their heads. Most of the tales were about animals, for the jungle was always at their door. The deer and the wild pig grubbed up their crops, and now and again the tiger carried off a man at twilight, within sight of the village gates.

Mowgli, who naturally knew something about what they were talking of, had to cover his face not to show that he was laughing, while Buldeo, the Tower musket across his knees, climbed on from one wonderful story to another, and Mowgli's shoulders shook with laughter.

Buldeo was explaining how the tiger that had carried away Messua's son was a ghost-tiger, and his body was inhabited by the ghost of a wicked, old money-lender, who had died some years ago. "And I know that this is true," he said, "because Purun Dass always limped from the blow that he got in a riot when his account books were burned, and we know that the tiger that I speak of limps, too, for the tracks of his pads are unequal."

"True, true, that must be the truth," said the graybeards, nodding together.

"All these tales are just cobwebs and foolishness!" said Mowgli. "That tiger limps because he was born lame, as everyone knows. To talk of the soul of a money-lender in a beast that never had the courage of a jackal is child's talk."

Buldeo was speechless with surprise for a moment, and the head-man stared.

"*Oho!* It is the jungle brat, is it?" said Buldeo. "If thou are so wise, better bring his hide to Khanhiwara, for the Government offered a hundred rupees for his life. Better still, talk not when thy elders speak."

Mowgli rose to go. "All the evening I have lain here listening," he called back over his shoulder, "and, except once or twice, Buldeo has not said one word of truth concerning the jungle, which is at his very doors. How, then, shall I believe the tales of ghosts and gods and goblins which he says he has seen?"

"It is full time that boy was put to work herding," said the head-man, while Buldeo puffed and snorted at Mowgli's impertinence.

The custom of most Indian villages is for a few boys to take the cattle and buffaloes out to graze in the early morning and bring them back at night. The very cattle that would trample a white man to death allow themselves to be banged and bullied and shouted at by children that hardly come up to their noses. As long as the boys stay with the herds, they are safe, for not even the tiger will charge a mob of cattle. But if they straggle to pick flowers or hunt lizards, they are sometimes carried off. Mowgli rode through the village street in the dawn, sitting on the back of Rama, the great herd bull. The slate-blue buffaloes, with their long, backward-sweeping horns and savage eyes, rose out their pens, one by one, and followed him, and Mowgli made it very clear to the children with him that he was the master. He beat the buffaloes with a long, polished bamboo stick, and told Kamya, one of the boys, to graze the cattle by themselves, while he went on with the buffaloes, and to be very careful not to stray away from the herd.

An Indian grazing ground is all rocks and scrub and little ravines, among which the herds scatter and disappear. The buffaloes generally keep to the pools and muddy places, where they lie wallowing or basking in the warm mud for hours. Mowgli drove them on to the edge of the plain; then he dropped from Rama's neck, trotted off to a bamboo clump, and found Gray Brother. "Ah," said Gray Brother, "I have waited here very many days. What is the meaning of this cattle-herding work?"

"It is an order," said Mowgli. "I am a village herder for a while. What news of Shere Khan?"

"He has come back to this country, and has waited here a long time for thee. Now he has gone off again, for game is scarce. But he means to kill thee."

"Very good," said Mowgli. "As long as he is away will thou or one of the four brothers sit on that rock, so that I can see thee as I come out of the village. When he comes back, wait for me in the ravine by the *dhak* tree in the center of the plain. We need not walk into Shere Khan's mouth."

Then Mowgli picked out a shady place, and lay down and slept while the buffaloes grazed round him. Herding in India is one of the laziest things in the world. The cattle move and crunch, and lie down, and move on again. They only grunt, and the buffaloes very seldom say anything, but get down into the muddy pools one after another, and work their way into the mud till only their noses and staring china-blue eyes show above the surface, and then they lie like logs. The sun makes the rocks dance in the heat, and the herd children hear one bird (never any more) whistling almost out of sight overhead. They know that if they died, or a cow died, that bird would sweep down, and the next bird miles away would see him drop and follow, and the next, and the next; and almost before they were dead, there would be a score of hungry birds coming out of nowhere. Then they sleep and wake and sleep again, and weave little baskets of dried grass and put grasshoppers in them. Or they catch two praying mantises and make them fight; or string a necklace of red and black jungle nuts; or watch a lizard basking on a rock, or a snake hunting a frog near the waters. Then they sing long, long songs with odd native sounds at the end of them, and the day seems longer than most people's whole lives. And perhaps they make a mud castle with mud figures of men and horses and buffaloes, and put reeds into the men's hands, and pretend that they are kings and the figures are their armies, or that they are gods to be worshiped. Then evening comes and the children return. And the buffaloes lumber up out of the sticky mud with noises like gunshots going off one after the other, and they all string across the gray plain back to the twinkling village lights.

Day after day Mowgli would lead the buffaloes out to the sticky mud where they stay, and day after day he would see Gray Brother's back a mile and a half away across the plain (so he knew that Shere Khan had not come back). And day after day he would lie on the grass listening to the noises round him, and dreaming of old days in the jungle. If Shere Khan had made a false step with his lame paw up in the jungles by the Waingunga, Mowgli would have heard him in those long, still mornings.

At last a day came when he did not see Gray Brother at the signal place, and he laughed and headed the buffaloes for the ravine by the *dhak* tree, which was all covered with golden-red flowers. There sat Gray Brother, every bristle on his back lifted.

"He has hidden for a month to throw thee off thy guard. He crossed the ranges last night with Tabaqui, hotfooted on thy trail," said the Wolf, panting.

Mowgli frowned. "I am not afraid of Shere Khan, but Tabaqui is very cunning."

"Have no fear," said Gray Brother, licking his lips a little. "I met Tabaqui in the dawn. Now he is telling all he knows to the birds, but he told me everything before I broke his back. Shere Khan's plan is to wait for thee at the village gate this evening—for thee and for no one else. He is lying up there now, in the big dry ravine of the Waingunga River."

"Has he eaten today, or does he hunt empty?" said Mowgli, for the answer meant life and death to him.

"He killed a pig at dawn, and he has drunk, too. Remember, Shere Khan could never fast, even for the sake of revenge."

"Oh! Fool, fool! He has eaten and drunk too, and he thinks that I shall wait till he has slept! Now, where does he lie? If there were but ten of us we might kill him as he lies. These buffaloes will not charge unless they catch his scent, and I cannot speak their language. Can we get behind his track so that they may smell it?"

"He swam far down the Waingunga to get rid of his scent," said Gray Brother.

"Tabaqui told him that, I know. He would never have thought of it alone." Mowgli stood with his finger in his mouth, thinking. "The big ravine of the Waingunga River. That opens out on the plain not half a mile from here. I can take the herd around through the jungle to the head of the ravine and then sweep down—but he would slink out at the foot. We must block that end. Gray Brother, can thou cut the herd in two for me?"

"Not I, perhaps—but I have brought a wise helper." Gray Brother trotted off and dropped into a hole. Then there lifted up a huge gray head that Mowgli knew well, and the hot air was filled with the most desolate cry of all the jungle—the hunting howl of a wolf at midday.

"Akela! Akela!" said Mowgli, clapping his hands. "I might have known that thou would not forget me. We have big work at hand. Cut the herd in two, Akela. Keep the cows and calves together, and the bulls and the buffaloes by themselves."

The two wolves ran, one after the other, in and out of the herd, which snorted and threw up its head, and separated into two clumps. In one, the cows stood with their calves in the center, and glared and pawed, ready, if a wolf would only stay still, to charge down and trample the life out of him. In the other, the bulls and the young bulls snorted and stamped, but though they looked more imposing, they were much less dangerous, for they had no calves to protect. No six men could have divided the herd so neatly.

"What do we do?" panted Akela. "They are trying to join again."

Mowgli slipped on to Rama's back. "Drive the bulls away to the left, Akela. Gray Brother, when we are gone, hold the cows together, and drive them into the foot of the ravine."

"How far?" said Gray Brother, panting and snapping.

"Till the sides are higher than Shere Khan can jump," shouted Mowgli. "Keep them there till we come down." The bulls swept off as Akela howled, and Gray Brother stopped in front of the cows. They charged down on him, and he ran just before them to the foot of the ravine, as Akela drove the bulls far to the left.

"Well done! Another charge and we're

almost there. Careful, now—careful, Akela. A snap too much and the bulls will charge. *Hujah!* This is wilder work than driving buck. Did thou think these creatures could move so swiftly?" Mowgli called.

"I have—have hunted these too in my time," gasped Akela in the dust. "Shall I turn them into the jungle?"

"Ay! Turn. Swiftly turn them! Rama is mad with rage. Oh, if I could only tell him what I need of him today."

The bulls were turned, to the right this time, and crashed into the standing thicket. The other herd children, watching with the cattle half a mile away, hurried to the village as fast as their legs could carry them, crying that the buffaloes had gone mad and run away.

But Mowgli's plan was simple enough. All he wanted to do was to make a big circle uphill and get to the top of the ravine, and then take the bulls down it and catch Shere Khan between the bulls and the cows. He knew that after a meal and a full drink Shere Khan would not be in any condition to fight or to clamber up the sides of the ravine. He was soothing the buffaloes now by voice, and Akela had dropped far to the rear, only whimpering once or twice to hurry the rear-guard. It was a long, long circle, for they did not wish to get too near the ravine and give Shere Khan warning. At last, Mowgli rounded up the bewildered herd at the head of the ravine on a grassy patch that sloped steeply down to the ravine itself. From that height you could see across the tops of the trees down to the plain below. But what Mowgli looked at was the sides of the ravine, and he saw with a great deal of satisfaction that they ran nearly straight up and down, while the vines and ivy that hung over them would give no foothold to a tiger who wanted to get out.

"Let them breathe, Akela," he said, holding up his hand. "Let them breathe. I must tell Shere Khan who comes. We have him in the trap."

He put his hands to his mouth and shouted down the ravine— it was almost like shouting down a tunnel—and the echoes jumped from rock to rock.

After a long time there came back the drawling, sleepy snarl of a fully-fed tiger just wakened.

"Who calls?" said Shere Khan, and a splendid peacock fluttered up out of the ravine screeching.

"I, Mowgli. Cattle thief, it is time to come

to the Council Rock! Down—hurry them down, Akela! Down, Rama, down!"

The herd paused for an instant at the edge of the slope, but Akela raised his voice in the full hunting-yell, and they pitched over one after the other, the sand and stones spurting up round them. Once started, there was no chance of stopping, and before they were squarely in the bed of the ravine Rama bellowed.

"Ha! Ha!" said Mowgli, on his back. "Now thou knowest!" and the torrent of black horns, foaming muzzles, and staring eyes whirled down the ravine just as boulders tumbled in a flood; the weaker buffaloes being shouldered out to the sides of the ravine where they tore through the hanging vines. They knew what the business was before them—the terrible charge of the buffalo herd against which no tiger can hope to stand.

Shere Khan heard the thunder of their hoofs, picked himself up, and lumbered down the ravine, looking from side to side for some way of escape, but the walls of the ravine went straight up, and he had to hold on, heavy with his dinner and his drink, willing to do anything rather than fight. The herd splashed through the pool he had just left, bellowing.

Mowgli heard an answering bellow from the foot of the ravine, and saw Shere Khan turn (the tiger knew if the worst came to the worst it was better to meet the bulls than the cows with their calves). Then Rama tripped, stumbled, and fell over something soft, and, with the bulls at his heels, crashed full into the other herd, while the weaker buffaloes were lifted clean off their feet by the shock of the meeting. That charge carried both herds out into the plain, goring and stamping and snorting. Mowgli waited for the right moment, and slipped off Rama's neck, running about him right and left with his stick.

"Quick, Akela! Break them up. Scatter them, or they will be fighting one another. Drive them away, Akela. *Hai*, Rama! *Hai, hai, hai!* my children. Softly now, softly! It is all over."

Akela and Gray Brother ran to and fro nipping the buffaloes' legs, and though the herd wheeled around once to charge up the ravine again, Mowgli managed to turn Rama, and the others followed him to the wallows.

Shere Khan needed no more trampling. He was dead, and the birds were coming for him already.

"Brothers, what a death!" said Mowgli,

feeling for the knife he always carried in a sheath around his neck now that he lived with men. "But he would never have fought. His hide will look well on the Council Rock. We must get to work swiftly."

A boy trained among men would never have dreamed of skinning a ten-foot tiger alone, but Mowgli knew better than anyone else how an animal's skin is fitted on, and how it can be taken off. But it was hard work, and Mowgli slashed and tore and grunted for an hour, while the wolves lolled out their tongues, or came forward and tugged as he ordered them. Presently a hand fell on his shoulder, and looking up he saw Buldeo with his musket. The children had told the village about the buffalo stampede, and Buldeo went out angrily, only too anxious to correct

Mowgli for not taking better care of the herd. The wolves dropped out of sight as soon as they saw the man coming.

"What is this folly?" said Buldeo angrily. "To think that thou can skin a tiger! Where did the buffaloes kill him? It is the Lame Tiger too. There is a reward of a hundred rupees on his head. Well, well, we will overlook thy letting the herd run off, and perhaps I will give thee one of the rupees of the reward when I have taken the skin to Khanhiwara." He fumbled in his waist cloth for flint and steel, and stooped down to singe Shere Khan's whiskers. Most native hunters singe a tiger's whiskers to prevent his ghost from haunting them.

"Hum!" said Mowgli, half to himself as he ripped back the skin of a forepaw. "So thou will take the hide to Khanhiwara for the reward, and perhaps give me one rupee? Now it is in my mind that I need the skin for my own use. *Heh!* Old man, take away that fire!"

"What kind of talk is this to the chief hunter of the village? Thy luck and the stupidity of thy buffaloes have helped thee to this kill. The tiger had just eaten, or he would have gone twenty miles by this time. Thou cannot even skin him properly, little beggar brat, and then I, Buldeo, must be told not to singe his whiskers. Mowgli, I will not give thee one bit of the reward, but only a very big beating. Leave the carcass!"

"By the Bull that bought me," said Mowgli, who was trying to get at the shoulder, "must I stay babbling to an old man all day? Here, Akela, this man plagues me."

Buldeo, who was still stooping over Shere Khan's head, found himself sprawling on the grass, with a gray wolf standing over him, while Mowgli went on skinning as though he were alone in all India.

"Ye-es," he said, between his teeth. "Thou art altogether right, Buldeo. Thou will never give me one bit of the reward. There is an old war between this lame tiger and myself—a very old war, and—I have won."

To do Buldeo justice, if he had been ten years younger he would have taken his chance with Akela had he met the wolf in the woods, but a wolf who obeyed the orders of this boy who had private wars with man-eating tigers was not a common animal. It was sorcery, magic of the worst kind, thought Buldeo, and he wondered whether the amulet around his neck would protect him. He lay as still as still, expecting every minute to see Mowgli turn into a tiger, too.

"Maharaj! Great King," he said at last in a husky whisper.

"Yes," said Mowgli, without turning his head, chuckling a little.

"I am an old man. I did not know that thou was anything more than a herdsboy. May I rise up and go away, or will thy servant tear me to pieces?"

"Go, and peace go with thee. Only, another time do not meddle with my game. Let him go, Akela."

Buldeo hobbled away to the village as fast as he could, looking back over his shoulder in case Mowgli should change into something terrible. When he got to the village he told a tale of magic and enchantment and sorcery that made the priest look very grave.

Mowgli went on with his work, but it was nearly twilight before he and the wolves had drawn the great skin clear of the body.

"Now we must hide this and take the buffaloes home! Help me to herd them, Akela."

The herd rounded up in the misty twilight, and when they got near the village, Mowgli saw lights, and heard the conches and bells in the temple blowing and banging. Half the village seemed to be waiting for him by the gate. "That is because I have killed Shere

Khan," he said to himself. But a shower of stones whistled about his ears, and the villagers shouted: "Sorcerer! Wolf's brat! Jungle demon! Go away! Leave quickly, or the priest will turn thee into a wolf again. Shoot, Buldeo, shoot!"

The old musket went off with a bang, and a young buffalo bellowed in pain.

"More sorcery!" shouted the villagers. "He can turn bullets. Buldeo, that was *thy* buffalo."

"Now what is this?" said Mowgli, bewildered, as the stones flew thicker.

"They are not unlike the Pack, these brothers of thine," said Akela, sitting down quietly. "It seems to me, if bullets mean anything, they would cast thee out."

"Wolf! Wolf's cub! Go away!" shouted the priest, waving a sprig of the sacred *tulsi* plant.

"Again? Last time it was because I was a man. This time it is because I am a wolf. Let us go, Akela."

A woman—it was Messua—ran across to the herd, and cried: "Oh, my son, my son! They say thou art a sorcerer who can turn himself into a beast at will. I do not believe this, but go away or they will kill thee. Buldeo says thou art a wizard, but I know thou has avenged Nathoo's death."

"Come back, Messua!" shouted the crowd. "Come back, or we will stone thee."

Mowgli laughed a little short ugly laugh, for a stone had hit him in the mouth. "Run back, Messua. This is one of the foolish tales they tell under the big tree at dusk. I have at least paid for thy son's life. Farewell—and run quickly, for I shall send the herd in more swiftly than they throw their brickbats. I am no wizard, Messua. Farewell!"

"Now, once more, Akela," he cried. "Bring the herd in."

The buffaloes were anxious enough to get to the village. They hardly needed Akela's yell, but charged through the gate like a whirlwind, scattering the crowd right and left.

"Keep count!" shouted Mowgli scornfully. "It may be that I have stolen one of them. Keep count, for I will do your herding no more. Fare you well, children of men, and thank Messua that I do not come in with my wolves and hunt you up and down your street."

He turned on his heel and walked away with the Lone Wolf. As he looked up at the stars, he felt happy. "No more sleeping in

traps for me, Akela. Let us get Shere Khan's
skin and go away. No, we will not hurt the village, for Messua was kind to me."

When the moon rose over the plain, making it look all milky, the horrified villagers saw
Mowgli, with two wolves at his heels and a
bundle on his head, trotting across at the
wolf's steady trot that eats up the long miles
like fire. Then they banged the temple bells
and blew the conches louder than ever. And
Messua cried, and Buldeo embroidered the
story of his adventures in the jungle, till he
ended by saying that Akela stood up on his
hind legs and talked like a man.

The moon was just going down when
Mowgli and the two wolves came to the hill of
the Council Rock, and they stopped at
Mother Wolf's cave.

"They have cast me out from the Man-
Pack, Mother," shouted Mowgli, "but I come
with the hide of Shere Khan to keep my
word."

Mother Wolf walked stiffly from the cave
with the cubs behind her, and her eyes glowed
as she saw the skin.

"I told him on that day, when he
crammed his head and shoulders into this
cave, hunting for thy life, Little Frog—I told

THE JUNGLE BOOK **111**

him that the hunter would be the hunted. It is well done."

"Little Brother, it is well done," said a deep voice in the thicket. "We were lonely in the jungle without thee," and Bagheera came running to Mowgli's bare feet. They clambered up the Council Rock together, and Mowgli spread the skin out on the flat stone where Akela used to sit, and pegged it down with four slivers of bamboo, and Akela lay down upon it, and called the old call to the Council, "Look—look well, O Wolves," exactly as he had called when Mowgli was first brought there.

Ever since Akela had been deposed, the Pack had been without a leader, hunting and fighting at their own pleasure. But they answered the call from habit. Some of them were lame from the traps they had fallen into, and some limped from shot wounds, and some were mangy from eating bad food, and many were missing. But they came to the Council Rock, all that were left of them, and saw Shere Khan's striped hide on the rock, and the huge claws dangling at the end of the empty dangling feet. It was then that Mowgli made up a song that came up into his throat all by itself, and he shouted it aloud, leaping up and down on the rattling skin, and beating time with his heels till he had no more breath left, while Gray Brother and Akela howled between the verses.

"Look well, O Wolves. Have I kept my word?" said Mowgli. And the wolves howled "Yes," and one tattered wolf howled:

"Lead us again, O Akela. Lead us again, O Man-cub, for we be sick of this lawlessness, and we would be the Free People once more."

"Nay," purred Bagheera, "that may not be. When ye are fully fed, the madness may come upon you again. Not for nothing are ye called the Free People. Ye fought for freedom, and it is yours. Enjoy it, O Wolves."

"Man-Pack and Wolf-Pack have cast me out," said Mowgli. "Now I will hunt alone in the jungle."

"And we will hunt with thee," said the four cubs.

So Mowgli went away and hunted with the four cubs in the jungle from that day on. But he was not always alone, because, years afterward, he became a man and married.

But that is a story for grown-ups.

AFTERWORD
by Beth Johnson

ABOUT THE AUTHOR

When Rudyard Kipling wrote about Indian forests and villages in *The Jungle Book*, he was writing about home. Kipling was born in Bombay, India, in 1865. He wasn't Indian, though; he was British. At that time, India was a British colony, and the Kiplings were one of many British families who had moved to India in hopes of making their fortune there. They had left England when Kipling's father had been offered a job teaching at a Bombay art school.

Kipling's early childhood seems to have been a very happy one. Even those British families who did not have much money could afford servants in India, and little Rudyard grew up being cared for by an *ayah* (an Indian nursemaid), a cook, and other people who helped around the house. He spent so much time with them that he learned Hindustani (the main language of India) before he learned English. Living among his Indian friends, hearing their stories, and soaking up the sounds and sights around him, he developed a deep love for India and its culture that he never lost. As an adult, he would set many of his finest pieces of writing there.

When Kipling was five years old, his life changed dramatically. India, with its hot climate, was home to dangerous tropical diseases. Also, there were not many British-style schools in India. For these reasons, many British parents at that time sent their children back to Great Britain to be educated. This is what happened to Kipling. His parents traveled with him to England and left him there, to be cared for by paid foster parents. He was desperately unhappy in his new home, and as an adult, he wrote bitterly about this period of life in several short stories.

When he was 12, Kipling left his foster home for a British boarding school where he was plunged into a wild, rowdy atmosphere of bullying, teasing, and practical jokes.

Kipling had poor eyesight and was never much of an athlete, but he earned the other boys' respect as a talented writer, became editor of the school newspaper, and made a handful of lifelong friends.

Although Kipling would have liked to attend college, his family couldn't afford to send him, so he returned to India at the age of 16 and started writing for a newspaper there. Covering local news taught the young journalist a great deal, and he soon became popular with readers. He began writing short stories in his spare time, many of them based on events he had witnessed as a reporter. Some of his stories were reprinted in a series of books called the Indian Railway Library, which were sold to travelers in railroad stations. Through the people who read them, Kipling's reputation began to spread across India and overseas. By the time Kipling moved back to England in 1889 and published his first novel, *The Light that Failed*, he was famous both in England and the U.S.

Kipling married an American woman, Carrie Balestier, and the couple lived for a while in Vermont. It was in Vermont that he drew on his childhood memories of India to write *The Jungle Book*. Note that the version of

The Jungle Book in your hands focuses exclusively on Mowgli's adventures, omitting several short stories that appear in Kipling's original book. The omitted stories include "The White Seal," "Rikki-Tikki-Tavi" (available from Townsend Press in *Great Stories of Suspense & Adventure*), "Toomai of the Elephants," and "Servants of the Queen" (also known as "Her Majesty's Servants").

Kipling's interest in writing for children was increased by the fact that he was now a father himself. He and Carrie had three children: Josephine, Elsie, and John. Sadly, only Elsie survived into adulthood. Josephine died of pneumonia when she was just a little girl. When the First World War broke out, John enlisted and was killed in his first battle. He was 18. To add to his parents' heartbreak, he was buried somewhere in France in an unmarked grave, which his parents were never able to locate. Both the Kiplings suffered deep depression over the loss of their son.

Despite his sadness, Kipling continued to be an extremely productive author for most of his life. He won the Nobel Prize for Literature in 1907, becoming the first British winner of that award.

Kipling's poetry is almost as well known

as his fiction. One of his best-known poems, called "My Boy Jack," recalls his sadness and pride over the son he sent to war and never saw again:

"Have you news of my boy Jack?"
Not this tide.
"When d'you think that he'll come back?"
Not with this wind blowing, and this tide.
"Has any one else had word of him?"
Not this tide.
For what is sunk will hardly swim,
Not with this wind blowing, and this tide.
"Oh, dear, what comfort can I find?"
None this tide,
Nor any tide,
Except he did not shame his kind—
Not even with that wind blowing, and that tide.
Then hold your head up all the more,
This tide,
And every tide;
Because he was the son you bore,
And gave to that wind blowing and that tide.

ABOUT *THE JUNGLE BOOK*

The Jungle Book helped make its author, Rudyard Kipling, world-famous after its publication in 1894. Readers—adults and children alike—responded enthusiastically to the story of little Mowgli. They delighted in his adventures in the jungle with Baloo and Bagheera and thrilled to the account of his battle with the wicked tiger Shere Khan. Almost a century later, the Disney movie version of *The Jungle Book* introduced Mowgli and his friends and enemies to a whole new generation of families.

What explains *The Jungle Book's* many years of popularity? There is more than one answer to that question, of course. But one of the secrets of its success is shared with another classic adventure book: *Tarzan of the Apes.* Written about twenty years after *The Jungle Book* (by Edgar Rice Burroughs), *Tarzan of the Apes* tells the story of an orphaned baby who is raised by great apes. Like Mowgli, Tarzan becomes a legendary leader within his new animal family.

The Jungle Book and *Tarzan of the Apes* are both fiction, of course. But they tap into people's fascination with a collection of stories that contain at least *some* truth. These are stories

about what are called "feral children"—
"wild" children raised without normal human
contact.

Growing up in India, a country rich in
legends of feral children, Kipling would have
been aware of such stories. His Indian *ayah*,
or nursemaid, may even have told them to
him. Maybe he dreamed about living in the
jungle himself, free as a wild animal, untrou-
bled by such ordinary concerns as school,
table manners, and everyday social behavior.

But whether Mowgli's experience in *The
Jungle Book* could really have happened or
not, it's still a marvelous reading adventure.
And that adventure owes a great deal to
Rudyard Kipling's skill with language. What a
wonderful writer he was! Reading his work is
like listening to a wise old grandfather who is
the best storyteller ever. He helps create that
sense of a cozy, comfortable relationship
when he speaks directly to the reader, like
this: "Now you must be content to skip ten or
eleven whole years, and only guess at the
wonderful life that Mowgli led among the
wolves, because if it were written out it would
fill ever so many books."

Did you notice Kipling's choice to use
old-fashioned language, including "thee" and

"thou," when the animals speak? Many readers would agree that his choice gives their speech a wonderful, poetic nobility:

> "And it is I, Raksha [The Demon], who answers. The man's cub is mine! He shall not be killed. He shall live to run with the Pack and to hunt with the Pack; and in the end, O hunter of little naked cubs—frog-eater—fish-killer—he shall hunt thee! Now go—go back to thy mother, burned beast of the jungle, lamer than thou came into the world! Go!"

In writing classes, students are often encouraged to "show, don't tell." Instead of just saying that a person is generous, they are told, it is more persuasive to show examples of that person's generosity. Kipling understood this concept very well. Here, he could have merely written that the monkeys were foolish and undisciplined. Instead, he shows that behavior, unforgettably:

> One of the monkeys made a speech and told his companions that Mowgli's capture marked a new thing in the history of the Bandar-log, for Mowgli was going to show them how to weave sticks and canes together as a protection against rain and cold. Mowgli picked up some vines and began to work them

in and out, and the monkeys tried to imitate; but in a very few minutes they lost interest and began to pull their friends' tails or jump up and down on all fours, coughing.

"I wish to eat," said Mowgli. "I am a stranger in this part of the jungle. Bring me food, or give me leave to hunt here."

Twenty or thirty monkeys bounded away to bring him nuts and wild pawpaws. But they ended up fighting on the road, and it was too much trouble to go back with what was left of the fruit.

But one of Kipling's greatest gifts as a writer was his ability to create wonderful metaphors. A metaphor is a word or phrase that describes somebody or something by comparing it to something else. When you call a person you dislike a "skunk," for instance, you are using a metaphor. Here, Kipling puts a metaphor into the mouth of Bagheera, who is telling Mowgli to go and get fire from the man-village:

> "Go down quickly to the men's huts in the valley, and take some of the Red Flower which they grow there, so that when the time comes thou may have even a stronger friend than I or Baloo or those of the Pack that love thee. Get the Red Flower."

Isn't "the red flower" a beautiful and imaginative way to describe fire? The way it "blooms" as it catches and flares up is, indeed, like a dramatic red flower. One other metaphor that Kipling creates is especially powerful:

> If you can imagine a lance, or a battering ram, or a hammer weighing nearly half a ton driven by a cool, quiet mind living in the handle of it, you can roughly imagine what Kaa was like when he fought.

A half-ton hammer with a "cool, quiet mind living in the handle of it"—what a chilling image, and what a perfect description of a cold, quiet, deadly python!

As you read Kipling, you will notice other examples of this great writer's talent. And you will undoubtedly be carried along with a plot that will keep you turning pages, for Kipling is not only a master of language; he is also a master storyteller.